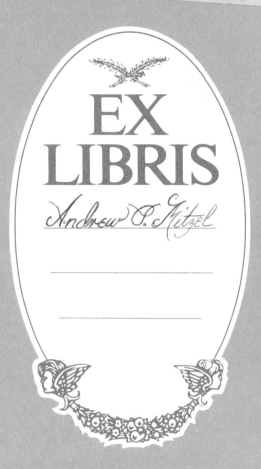

EX LIBRIS

Andrew P. Mitzel

Fleur stiffened, realizing that Alain was obviously suffering from acute embarrassment.

"When I proposed marriage," he said, "I believed you were a middle-aged spinster stuck in the middle of nowhere, at the beck and call of your father, and with no hope of ever escaping that rut.

"No one thought to mention that you were a young and lovely girl who probably could have had the choice of half a dozen men. I simply don't understand why you agreed to my proposal—tying yourself to a blind man!"

Fleur's heart beat madly. He must never know the foolish dreams she had woven around him!

CHATEAU OF FLOWERS

The Romantic Story of Lily of the Valley

Strand.

Margaret Rome

CHATEAU OF FLOWERS

The Romantic Story of
Lily of the Valley

Harlequin Books
TORONTO · LONDON · NEW YORK · AMSTERDAM · SYDNEY · HAMBURG · PARIS

CHATEAU
OF FLOWERS

The Romantic Story of
Lily of the Valley

Chapter One

THE GARDEN LAY SOMNOLENT under the pressing blanket of an August heat wave. Flowers breathed out their perfume at only half-strength, biding their time until a shower of rain should release the full symphony of their scent. The buzz of a fat, furry-coated bee was the only noise audible in the still air, and even that was forced: a tired, monotonous sound that seemed to end on a relieved sigh when the bee alighted on the petulant lip of a drooping antirrhinum.

Idly, Fleur Maynard watched it disappear into the mouth of the flower, her hands ceasing momentarily their task of shelling peas into a basin balanced on her lap. How peaceful it all was. She leaned back in her chair and pushed aside a wave of hair that had fallen across her eyes. Peace! But did she want peace? Forever, it seemed, her life had run on a placid, unalterable course: no heartaches, no shattering disappointments, not even a minor tragedy had disturbed the smooth pattern of her existence—and no excitement either. A small smile curved her lips at a fleeting thought. How would her father's parishioners react to the knowledge that the girl they regarded as their minister's right hand, the quiet, unobtrusive child they had watched grow up into a serene, uncomplicated young woman content to help out at parish functions, to step into the breach when a babysitter was required or an old person needed nursing, did, in reality, yearn for a more exciting life, yearned to cross the boundaries of the sleepy Surrey village where she had lived all her life into the vast world that beckoned from outside?

Her mother stirred in the adjacent deck chair and opened one sleepy eye. "Is your father back yet, dear?" she questioned, her face a picture of dawning concern. Fleur smiled. The devotion her parents showed toward one another never failed to please and reassure her.

Although they were both well past middle age their love was, if anything, stronger than it had been in their youth. Her mother still blushed charmingly when her husband paid her a compliment and he, in turn, was not averse to being told by her how wonderful he was and how lucky the people of the village of Gillingham were to have him as their vicar. They were both such lovable innocents, Fleur had decided long ago. They saw evil in no one and the worst of villains received from them the benefit of the doubt and was never condemned. Perhaps that was why even the most hardened individual left the vicarage with a grateful smile and a renewed hope in human nature, and perhaps that was why Fleur often found herself fussing over her parents with the same concern she felt for the youngsters in her Brownie pack.

There was an unconscious note of maternal soothing in her voice when she answered. "Now, mother, don't worry. Father is a little late, but today is his day for visiting the hospital, and you know how involved he gets with the patients, especially any new arrivals. He'll be home soon, I'm sure of it."

When the veil of disturbance lifted from her mother's eyes, Fleur stood up, handed her the

basin of shelled peas, then began to stretch
long and luxuriously to rid herself of the stiff-
ness brought about by her prolonged inactiv-
ity. "Ah, that's better! It was lovely while it
lasted, but lazing simply doesn't agree with
me, mother!"

Jean Maynard smiled and looked up at her
lovely, laughing daughter, wondering again at
the stroke of fortune that had brought them a
child long after she and her husband had given
up hope of ever having children. And such a
child. They had named her well: she was as
lovely as any of the flowers surrounding her in
the old-fashioned garden. With maternal
wonder she noted again Fleur's petal-soft skin,
matt white and unblemished, her full, sensitive
mouth the color of wild roses, and the fascinating, deep pansy blue of her eyes. Hair the
color of pale wheat fell in heavy waves onto
shoulders so slim they seemed incapable of
bearing its weight, but the stem of her green-
clad body was supple with health, and youthful
curves gave promise of a voluptuousness to
come. But to Malcolm and Jean Maynard the
most comforting knowledge of all was the
knowledge of the beauty within. Fleur's nature
was so sweet and so abundantly generous she
was loved by all, even though—her mother

permitted herself an impish smile—she gave at times the impression of being a thoroughly modern little lady who felt responsible for the unworldliness of her parents and who carried the troubles of the village on her own straight back.

When Fleur raised an inquiring eyebrow, her mother masked her smile and rose to her feet to turn in the direction of the house. "I'll begin preparing dinner, dear, if you go and change. By the time it's ready your father should be home." Fleur nodded agreement and wound her arm through her mother's as they walked together back to the house.

When the Reverend Malcolm Maynard arrived home an hour later dinner was ready to be served and his wife and daughter were waiting to welcome him. But as soon as he entered the house they were both immediately aware that something was wrong. A frown creased his usually unfurrowed brow, and the twinkle they were used to seeing in his placid eyes had been replaced by deep seriousness. Malcolm Maynard had a heart big enough to contain the troubles of all who sought his help, his calling was as worn as a cloak of compassion under which every mortal was offered shelter, but he tried at all times to keep a sense of proportion so that neither he nor his family was overwhelmed by the misery he encountered in his work. But this time he was troubled—so troubled he could not even try to pretend.

"Malcolm, my dear—" his wife moved toward him "—is something wrong? What has happened?"

Fleur did not attempt to question him. It was at such times as these she realized how superfluous she was to her parents' happiness. They loved her dearly, and she knew they would have been horrified at the thought of her feeling shut out, but they were two halves of a whole and when trouble descended upon one the burden was immediately shouldered by the other.

Malcolm shook his head and instead of moving to the dining room where his meal was waiting, he crossed over to the small room he used as a study and sank down into his leather armchair. He waited until his wife and Fleur had joined him and when they were both seated opposite, showing an anxiety they could not hide, he began to explain.

"I've had a most distressing time at the hospital this afternoon!" With a boyish gesture of puzzlement he ran his fingers through his gray hair. "Heaven knows, I've visited hundreds of patients in the Royal Southern Hospital, many of them blind and without a hope of ever regaining their sight, but *this* young man—" his voice deepened with distress "—is in such utter solitude! He'll allow no one to comfort him, he rejects all offers of friendship and, or so he tells me, he has no faith whatsoever in either surgeons or priests!"

His wife leaned forward to give his hand a comforting pat. "Tell us about it from the beginning, my dear; you'll feel much better when you've got it all off your chest."

"It isn't what I feel that matters, Jean," he answered fiercely. "I simply must find some way of helping this young man!"

Wisely, his wife remained silent and after drawing a deep breath he took her advice and began again. "When I reached the hospital this afternoon there was a message waiting for me from Sir Frank Hamlin, the famous eye surgeon. No doubt you'll remember hearing me speak of him before—he sends most of his patients to the Royal Southern for treatment. Sir Frank requested that I speak with him before going up to the wards, so naturally I sought him out to find out what he wanted."

Fleur leaned forward, anxious not to miss any of her father's low-spoken words. "Sir Frank asked my help in connection with a patient just recently admitted—a young Frenchman whose family is very close to his. The story he told me of the young man's accident was tragic. Two years ago he was blinded by acid. For all of those two years the doctors in France gave him hope, but very faint hope. Then, after six unsuccessful operations, his family contacted Sir Frank, who immediately had him transported to England—to the Royal Southern. Just after the accident the young man had great trust in his doctors. He never complained of the pain and discomfort, which must have been considerable, because after each operation he was convinced he would see again. But gradually his optimism faltered and was replaced by bitterness until, after the last abortive operation, he sank into such despair he vowed he would never allow himself to be operated on again."

"Oh, the poor, dear boy," Jean Maynard murmured, close to tears.

The vicar nodded. "Yes, he is certainly to be pitied."

"But what did Sir Frank want you to do, Father?" Fleur queried gravely.

"He wanted to enlist my help in reviving the young man's spirits, my dear. Sir Frank is almost certain he can operate successfully and he is most anxious to try. The young man's

family has managed to persuade him to under-
go just one more operation and although he
was very reluctant to do so, he agreed. But it is
his mental attitude that is so worrying. Sir
Frank insisted it would be futile to operate on
any patient in such a state of mind. That is why
he has asked for my help in trying to revive the
young man's optimism. Sir Frank himself has
tried, and so has the patient's family—but
without success. I'm afraid I'm being looked
upon as a last desperate hope."

His head sank down upon his chest in a
gesture of such defeat his wife had to remonstrate. "But you can do it, my dear, I know
you can! How many such people have you
managed to comfort, and how many of them
have returned to thank you for your help?"

The vicar shook his head. "I've tried," he
told her simply, "and failed. Never before have
I encountered such deep, bitter resentment,
such cold, impenetrable indifference. For all of
an hour I tried to penetrate the armor with
which he has surrounded himself, but the only
return for my efforts was an occasional cold
smile and then finally the remark I repeated
earlier: 'I'm sorry, but I'm afraid I have no
faith whatsoever in either surgeons or priests!'
Nor in any other form of humanity, I'll
wager," the vicar stated unhappily. "The man

has turned into an insensible automaton. I feel he has been hurt so often—and perhaps not merely physically—that he has determined never to allow himself to feel ever again!"

There was an aghast silence as each of them tried to imagine the extent of hurt necessary to cause such complete withdrawal. For all of five minutes no one spoke, then, on a small eager breath, Jean Maynard suggested, "Fleur might be able to help. . . ."

Fleur's head jerked up. "Me? What on earth could I do? Really, father . . . ." But when she turned to appeal for his support she saw with dismay that his eyes had brightened with renewed hope.

"Of course!" His mouth relaxed into a slow smile. "Why didn't I think of that? It's certainly worth a try!"

"No, father, I couldn't. . . ."

All during dinner Fleur argued. She felt petrified at the idea of even meeting the man her father had described and was appalled at the thought of the reception she might receive from him if he should decide to treat any effort on her part as the gross impertinence it surely would be. But her parents became so upset by her adamant refusals she finally felt forced to give in, and when she went up to her room that evening she was committed to a promise to approach the fierce young Frenchman the very next day.

The following afternoon she left for the hospital early. It was her day for helping out in the wards: taking around the telephone trolley, writing and reading letters for patients in the ophthalmic wards, making lists of things asked for that could not be supplied by the Women's Auxiliary trolley and generally making herself useful. But today she felt the need to talk to someone before approaching the patient she had promised to see, and who better, she thought, than her friend Jennifer Dalton, a staff nurse at the hospital, who by chance was at present working on that ward.

She found her sitting in the ward nurse's small office drinking a cup of tea and puzzling over some reports she had strewn across the desk. After a diffident knock, Fleur popped her head around the door and asked, "Have you a spare minute, Jennifer?"

Jennifer pushed aside the papers and welcomed her with enthusiasm. "Come in, Fleur, you've turned up at exactly the right moment; I was just beginning to feel a scream coming on! Honestly, the way these juniors' reports have been written one could be forgiven for thinking they'd been transcribed by a martian! Can I get you a cup of tea?" she rushed on, pulling a chair forward.

"No, thanks." Fleur sank despondently into the proffered seat. "It's advice I want."

Jennifer's eyes assessed Fleur's anxious face, then with a hint of exasperation she accused her, "Must you burden yourself with the problems of every lame dog you meet, Fleur?" Fleur's mouth opened to protest, but Jennifer held up her hand and conceded, "Oh, don't tell me, I know, this time it's different!" She leaned forward to give emphasis to her next words. "Each time it's different, and each time the results are the same. You worry yourself to a frazzle over some individual who doesn't deserve your help and who, indeed, might benefit from being left to sort out his own affairs. When are you going to start thinking about yourself? That's what I want to know!"

Fleur was not put off by her friend's abrupt speech, for she knew her too well. At first sight the two girls looked unlikely candidates for friendship. But Fleur's shy, retiring nature needed the pushing and prodding of Jennifer's ebullience, and although sometimes overwhelmed by it, she was often glad to seek her positive advice.

"I haven't come here to talk about me," Fleur stated firmly.

"All right—" Jennifer leaned back in her chair with a look of resigned patience "—tell me the worst, who is it this time?"

"Your new patient," Fleur admitted. "Father asked me to call on him today to try to cheer him up, and I was hoping perhaps you could give me some idea what subjects he finds interesting. I'm at a loss to know what to talk to him about."

Jennifer jerked to attention and shrieked, "You don't mean our French Count?"

Fleur laughed, "Oh, is that what you call him. . . ."

Jennifer rushed into words without heeding the question. "My dear, every nurse on this ward has tried to get through to him! Mean, moody, magnificent—we've run out of adjectives! Half the staff hate him and the rest are in love with him, but on one point we're all agreed—he's impossible!"

Fleur's heart sank. Her father's words had prepared her up to a point, but that Jennifer, forthright, unfearing Jennifer, should stand in awe of him made him sound even more formidable. She cleared her throat and censured gently, "He *is* blind, Jennifer."

Jennifer's face went grim. "Yes, but so are most of the other patients in this ward, and they don't have private suites and the undivided attention of Sir Frank Hamlin to help soften the blow. The young man's spoiled, Fleur, make no mistake about that, and although he has lost his sight he's by no means incapacitated otherwise. It's extraordinary how quickly he senses pity and his arrogant rejection of it can be devastating. Don't expose yourself to the lash of his tongue, please, Fleur. Leave him to those experienced enough and hard enough to cope, because you're simply not equipped to handle him!"

Fleur blanched, but she shook her head and answered firmly, "I must see him. I promised father I would and I can't go back on that promise. When will be the most convenient time?"

Jennifer threw up her hands in despair. "All right, if you've made up your mind, then on your own head be it!" She softened when Fleur's shoulders drooped. "Look, you haven't been around the wards yet, have you?" Fleur shook her head. "Good!" Jennifer answered. "Then by the time you've finished doing that it should be teatime. Sir Frank will have visited his patient long before then, and I'll see to it he's left severely alone so that when you do go in he might be so sick of his own company he'll welcome any visitor. How will that do?"

"Well, thank you for nothing!" Fleur drew herself up with dignity and made toward the door. Jennifer's laughter was still ringing in her ears as she walked quickly down the corridor to collect the telephone trolley. Her lips quirked a little as her sense of humor responded to her friend's quip, but it faded fast when she began to contemplate the ordeal that loomed only a couple of short hours away.

Chapter Two

FLEUR DID NOT KNOW whether to feel relieved or sorry when the time for her visit drew near. All afternoon while she had ministered to the patients in the main ward her eyes had been drawn to the curtained window behind which was the private room housing the man she had promised to visit. Her thoughts had been so chaotic she had found it quite impossible to concentrate on the tasks she had been given, and this had caused much good-natured chaffing from the patients—many of whom were now friends of long standing. But she had managed to struggle through, and now, as she pushed the telephone trolley back into its

22

alcove and nervously smoothed down her hair, she began to feel the stirring of very real panic.

Slowly, she walked down the corridor until she was outside the room; then, bracing herself as if to do battle, she tapped lightly on the door.

"*Entrez!*" she was brusquely commanded.

Three hesitant steps took her inside the room. Her eyes went immediately toward the bed and found it unoccupied, its covers drawn back to reveal uncreased sheets and crisp white pillows. Along the opposite wall was a window that looked out onto the hospital grounds and standing immobile in front of it was the tall figure of a man wearing a dark jewel-colored dressing gown of heavy silk. Fleur's heart somersaulted, then began to pound with hard, painful throbs. Without flickering an eyelash, she traced his portrait indelibly upon her memory, so that when she was alone she might take it out and look at it again and again. He looked so attractive standing there with the light from the partially curtained window lancing down upon his dark head that it was no wonder Fleur's unawakened heart responded with romantic fervor at her first sight of him. He was a cavalier in modern clothing, his face dark and brooding, his chin severely out-thrust—a sign of obstinacy—eyes screened but

exciting, his nose blade-straight but with
flaring nostrils that warned he sensed
approaching danger . . . or interference. All he
lacked was a colorful doublet, a swinging cape
and a long, thin rapier to hang against the lean
length of his leg. He was a hero of Cervantes.
Like Don Quixote who took windmills for
giants and sheep for armies, he gave the
impression that he would consider a friendly
overture a provocation and pity or concern an
insult.

"Well?" His impatient voice challenged the
silent room. "Who are you and what do you
want?"

Compassion filled her at this reminder of his
blindness and it was all she could do to keep
her voice steady when she faltered, "I . . . I'm
Fleur Maynard, the Reverend Mr. Maynard's
daughter—he visited you yesterday, if you remember?"

He tilted his haughty head and without
turning away from the window brusquely
asked, "You mean that fool of a priest? I
thought I had made it quite plain to him that
his presence was superfluous, so why, I
wonder, has he sent me his daughter? Perhaps
he would like you to guide me around the
grounds and so dispense with my white stick,

24

or—ah yes, I have it—he wants you to teach me braille, a worthy occupation for a vicar's daughter!"

If he had mocked her she could have forgiven him; his sarcasm could have fallen upon her own head and she would not have flinched. But to hear her kind, gentle-hearted father so maligned was more than she could bear. With the primitive instinct of a mother tiger defending her young she turned on him.

"I find your morbid self-pity abhorrent, *monsieur*! Now I understand why people prefer to leave you alone with your unhealthy thoughts and childish tantrums!"

Her spurt of temper faded into an appalled silence. He did not speak, but his fist clenched tightly and hovered momentarily over the hilt of a nonexistent rapier. Although silent, his anger could be felt in the quiet room. No one, she guessed, had ever spoken to the arrogant Frenchman that way before and he had found it most indigestible; if she had been a man she felt sure he would have struck her! Her whole body trembled as she waited, too ashamed and frightened to run toward the door. Hot color rushed to her cheeks, then receded, leaving her eyes enormous in her white face. Just when she thought she would crack under the strain, he relaxed his tense body and turned around to face her. With a meekness she would not have believed possible he apologized.

"You are quite right, *mademoiselle*, I have become impossible to live with. You are not the only one who thinks so. My temper gets beyond control, but I know of no way to remedy this. Perhaps—" his voice became silky "—if you were to help me . . . ?" He must have heard her dismayed gasp, because his voice became charged with mocking sarcasm. "Come now, vicar's daughter, where is your charity? You know you dare not refuse me for your father's sake, for how would he react to the knowledge that his daughter had denied help to a desperate man?"

Immediately, a picture of her father's anxious face flashed before her eyes and the refusal she was about to utter faltered into silence. He was clever, this Frenchman; unerringly he had hit upon the one thing that could influence her in his favor. If she were to refuse his request her father would be hurt far more than he would.

"In what way can I help, *monsieur*? There are people far better qualified than I just waiting for your command, so why not let *them* help you?" she questioned stiffly.

He moved away from the window, and

using her voice as a directive, walked toward her. Only a step away he stopped, so close she could have reached out and touched him. It was hard to believe he could not see, so sure were his movements. His steady, unfathomable eyes were trained upon her face as if taking in every detail of her features, so much so that a blush began to rise under her skin. It was only when she saw the faint white scars on his eyelids and brow—denoting recent plastic surgery—that she was able to believe it, and then her blush deepened with an onrush of shame.

"Why you?" he queried, suddenly harsh. "Simply because you are the first person I have spoken to since my accident who is honest enough to tell me the truth about myself! For two years I have been consistently lied to and I'm heartily sick of it! Hearing you speak so frankly was like a breath of air reaching me through clouds of stifling commiserations and supposedly soothing platitudes. You are the one person I would trust to speak the truth to me always and for that reason I do not intend to lose sight of you. You will have to humor me, vicar's daughter, because if you do not I shall refuse to let them operate! What is your answer to that? Are you agreeable?"

"Agree to blackmail?" Fleur choked. "Does

one ever have a choice in such circumstances?"

He shrugged and turned to walk back to the
window. Standing in a shaft of sunlight, he
lifted his face to let the light play upon his
scars, seeming to enjoy the warm, delicate
touch upon his tormented eyes. Then, realizing she was waiting for an answer, he told her
with sudden irritability, "No, you have no
choice! I did not ask to become the target of
your overdeveloped sense of duty, so I cannot
therefore be charged with taking advantage of
it!" Suddenly he tired of her. "Go now, I want
to rest, but be back here tomorrow in time to
have lunch with me."

Rigid with anger at her ignominious dismis-
sal, she marched out of the room, only just
resisting the urge to slam the door.

SIR FRANK WAS AMAZED and delighted at the
change in his patient after just a couple of
weeks of Fleur's company. Jennifer expressed
the view that Fleur had achieved the impossible when, instead of brooding in his room,
her patient began to demand more and more
outings in Sir Frank's chauffeur-driven car
with Fleur acting as his eyes, painting word
pictures of the countryside as they journeyed
through it. Malcolm Maynard was jubilant

and so proud of his daughter he could not find words enough to praise her. But the strain Fleur was undergoing was visible to her mother; only she began to rejoice less as she compared the young Frenchman's restored spirits with the subdued aura of disquiet surrounding Fleur—brought on, Mrs. Maynard had no doubt, by his heavy demands upon her time.

She tried to remonstrate with Fleur about this one afternoon as she watched her get ready for yet another outing. "Fleur dear, you look tired. Why don't you rest this afternoon and I'll telephone the hospital to tell them you don't feel up to escorting Monsieur Treville to the races?"

Fleur was in the act of pulling a pink cotton dress over her head and her reply was muffled, but audible. "I'm not a bit tired, mother, so please don't fuss." When her head emerged from the dress she continued firmly, "Besides, Alain will be most disappointed if I let him down. He's very fond of horse racing and was quite excited when I mentioned there was a meeting to be held nearby. I couldn't possibly let him down now, could I?"

Her mother sighed. "That's all very well, Fleur, but I'm beginning to worry about you. You don't display half the energy you used to and you look so pale. Alain Treville is a charming young man and a most considerate one otherwise, but he's so possessive! You haven't been away from him for more than a few hours since the first day you met him. Are you sure it isn't all becoming too much for you?"

Fleur turned away to hide the quick spurt of tears her mother's words had precipitated. It was just as well her parents thought Alain Treville charming and considerate. To them he was, but only she knew of the black depression that often overtook him when they were alone together. She had learned to keep silent while he ranted and railed against the fates that had blinded him. She had become his safety valve—his whipping boy. To everyone at the hospital he was now a model patient, easy to please and very cooperative; she was the one who bore the brunt of the devils that roused within him a despair so violent that only by lashing out at another could he achieve relief. At first when these moods had overtaken him she had answered him back sharply, but this had tended to aggravate him still further and after flinching under his stinging tongue on half a dozen occasions she had decided to opt for the line of least resistance and to sit quietly until his spleen was spent. But there had been a few occasions when he had been sweet, so heart-stirringly charming she would have denied him nothing, and it was on the last of these occasions that she had realized she had fallen in love with him.

"Fleur!" Her mother was still waiting for an answer, so she went across and knelt at her feet.

"Mother, Sir Frank confided in me that he hopes to operate on Alain some time next week, so I won't be wanted much longer. When he regains his sight he'll go back to France and in time he'll forget all about me." Her heart jerked painfully, but she forced herself to go on. "In a few weeks everything will be back to normal and I'll have plenty of time to rest, but as long as he needs me I must be with him, do you understand?"

Her mother patted her hand, understanding more than Fleur intended. "Very well, my dear, I'll say no more. Just remember—" she hesitated, then continued slowly "—your happiness is very important to us and anything you might decide to do will be accepted by your father and myself as being necessary to that happiness."

Fleur hugged her. "What possible decision could I be called upon to make that would affect my life with you and father?" She laughed lightly. Her mother just smiled and stood up to go toward the door, but when she had left the room Fleur remained kneeling by the bed, reflecting upon her words.

Sir Frank's car was late arriving. Alain was already inside and through her open bedroom window Fleur heard her mother's voice pleading with him not to get out as she was sure she, Fleur, would be down in a matter of seconds. Alain's pleasantly accented voice said something in reply but she did not wait to listen. Grabbing her handbag, she ran down the stairs and outside to the waiting car, eager to discover whether this was to be one of his good days, or, heaven forbid, whether she was to endure more hours of deliberate crucifixion from his searing tongue.

But she knew at first sight of him that it was to be a happy day; his mouth relaxed into an involuntary smile of welcome when he heard her approach and, although they were screened by dark glasses, she sensed there were no shadows in the eyes that swung with uncanny perception to her flushed face. "Are you ready, Fleur?" he questioned, impatient to be on his way.

"Yes, Alain," she replied, her tongue stumbling over his name. He had insisted, on the day she had been commanded to lunch with him, that they dispense with formality and use first names, but it had taken him the better part of a week to persuade her to drop Monsieur Treville in favor of Alain.

"Good. Then let us be on our way—we must not miss the first race!"

It was ideal weather for such an outing, pleasantly warm with a light breeze preventing it from becoming oppressively hot. They found a quiet vantage point—he did not like crowds—but one that gave Fleur a comprehensive view of the racetrack. When they were settled Alain dismissed the chauffeur, telling him he was free to enjoy himself in his own way until the time arranged for the return journey.

Although Fleur knew nothing about racing, she had an instinctive grasp of what would interest Alain. She described everything around her in such detail that he became absorbed, and when the racing actually started her commentary was so crisp and accurate that his face glowed with enjoyment. Between races she shared the food from the lunch basket they had brought with them—flaky sausage rolls, sandwiches of delicious pink ham, slivers of chicken breast, fruit and a bottle of sparkling wine that had been chilled, then packed in a thermos container to retain its refreshing tang.

When they had finished eating Alain lay back upon the rug they had spread upon the grass and told her with a relaxed sigh, "That was wonderful! Thank you for a most enjoyable afternoon, Fleur. When I get back home you must come to visit me and I'll take you to the races!"

Her heart lifted. It was the first time he had mentioned his home or, indeed, anything about himself. She would have liked to ask, but had been too afraid of being snubbed. In his present mood, however, she decided to chance it.

"Where is your home, Alain?" she asked diffidently.

A frown flickered across his face, then was gone. "Near Grasse," he answered abruptly. Then as reluctant memory overtook him, he elaborated, "Grasse, as you probably know, is the center of the French perfume industry, a region known as the garden of France. All the year round the flowers bloom along the Mediterranean coast—from Menton to Hyeres they flower in infinite profusion. Cannes is famous for its roses, acacia and jasmine, Nîmes for its thyme, rosemary and lavender, Nice for violets and mignonette. But of all of them the most famous is Grasse, because there we grow the most flowers and it is there the perfumes are manufactured."

She was fascinated. No wonder he reveled in the touch of the sun when he had lived his life in such a paradise! "Flowers all the year round?" Unconsciously she had repeated the phrase that had so caught her fancy.

"But yes." Alain nodded. "Every single month of the year. From January to March there are violets, lilies of the valley, jonquils and mimosa; during April, May and June, roses, and in June also we have the mignonette, pinks and golden broom. This month, the coast will be a riot of lavender, jasmine and tuberoses, then in August, September and October we will have mint, geranium and acacia. Even at Christmastime all districts are turned into a sea of yellow when the cassia blooms, sending scent wafting for miles around."

"Oh, stop!" Fleur laughingly admonished him. "My mind simply cannot absorb any more! How fortunate you are to have such beauty to go back to, and how you must be dying to see it all again!"

She could have bitten out her tongue the moment the words were spoken, but it was too late. He made no physical movement, but instinctively she felt his withdrawal. Anxiously, her eyes searched his face, trying to probe behind the screen of dark glasses, but he betrayed nothing. His lithe, slim body seemed relaxed until she noticed his clenched fists, the knuckles standing out white against brown skin, betraying his tenseness.

Full of remorse, she reached out and covered his fist with her hand. Earnestly, aware of his agony, she assured him, "You will see again, Alain, I know you will! You mustn't allow despair to mar your chance of success, because it's vitally important that you are relaxed and in good spirits when Sir Frank operates next week."

Her hand was rejected with hard fury as he hissed through clenched teeth, "*Mon Dieu!* Don't humor me! What do you know of operations? Haven't I endured six of them, six abortive, agonizing attempts to make me see again? 'Don't worry,' " he mimicked, " 'the scars around your eyes are healing nicely!' What do I care about scars when all I want is my sight!"

Fleur's breath caught in a hard sob. Willing herself to withstand the lash of his anger because of the relief he found in venting his frustrations upon her, she fought desperately not to let his dejection take root in her own mind. She could not bear even to think what he might do if he were ever to be told there was no hope, that he was to be blind for the rest of his life.

Depression kept her silent as she gathered up the remains of their meal and repacked the basket. Alain had retreated once more into his shell of moody aloofness and nothing she might say would bring him out of it. She began praying inwardly that the following week would pass quickly. Physically, she was strong, but how much longer could her tortured spirit withstand the punishment she had elected to bear in order to help Alain Treville achieve his heart's desire?

Chapter Three

THE OPERATION WAS OVER. Jennifer had whisked
into the waiting room only minutes before to
tell Fleur that Alain was being brought back to
his room and that Sir Frank wanted to have a
word with her. She was filled with foreboding.
Had the operation been unsuccessful? Could it
be that Sir Frank was going to ask her to
break bad news?

She paced the floor in an agony of doubt as
the minutes ticked by and Sir Frank did not
appear. The operation had taken hours to perform and all the time she had waited, hoping
her nearness would in some way be communicated to Alain so that he might be comforted

38

by it. But now she wanted to see him, to assure herself that he was not in pain.

The door opened and Sir Frank entered, his face drawn with fatigue. "Ah, Miss Maynard, thank you for waiting. I did especially want to have a word with you!" As he pulled up a chair and waited for her to be seated she scanned his face and saw beneath the gray tiredness signs of very real worry. Her hands plucked nervously at her skirt as she waited for his next words.

"The corneal graft has been made on his right eye," he told her gravely, "and I intended within the next few days to do the left one. You realize, of course—as does Alain—that the operation has to be done in two parts?" When she nodded, he continued, "After operating on the right eye I examined the left one very carefully. . . ." She stiffened when his voice faltered into silence.

"And?" she urged.

He dropped into a seat before admitting reluctantly, "I'm afraid the outlook is not very promising."

"You mean the operation was not a success—that Alain will not regain his sight?"

He hesitated, searching for words to soften the blow. "The left eye is the more badly injured of the two, but even so I had felt confident that it was not irreparably damaged. Today, however, I found signs of infection. We must reduce this infection before continuing and this will mean postponing the second operation until it is completely cleared up. That is why I asked to speak to you, my dear. You have worked such miracles with Alain these past few weeks that I wanted to be sure you'll be there when he needs you—as he surely will do when I tell him of my decision."

As if through a fog Fleur heard his voice sounding the death knell of Alain's hopes. Was it for this he had endured seven torturing operations?

Would it not have been kinder to have left him altogether without hope than to inflict upon his volatile nature the seesaw of emotional strain that, more than anything else, was the cause of his moods of despair?

Tearfully, she challenged Sir Frank, "Why didn't you leave well enough alone? Why tantalize him with further promises that he might see when you know there's no hope?"

Gently, Sir Frank contradicted her, "There is always hope, my dear. We doctors have to believe that or we would never operate. I'm as depressed as you by this setback, but I implore you to believe that it is just a setback . . . and to help Alain to believe it, too. In a year—even less—it will be possible for me to finish the operation, this time successfully, but I need you to help me convince Alain that things are not as hopeless as they might seem. Can I count on that help?"

"He'll never agree," she answered through cold lips. "With Alain it's a case of now or never, I'm certain of that."

Sir Frank's shoulders sagged as if hearing what he feared put into words made the fact concrete. "Then God help him and his family to endure the consequences! His mother is a very dear friend of mine, as was his late father, and I would have liked nothing better than to succeed in restoring their son's sight, but if what you say is true I shall never achieve that goal."

His despondency was very moving and Fleur responded to it by promising tearfully, "I'll do my very best to make him understand, Sir Frank, but if he refuses to listen please don't blame yourself. Later, when he's had time to overcome his disappointment, perhaps he'll consider trying again."

He reached out to pat her hand. "You're a sweet child. I'm not surprised my patient found comfort in your presence and I'm certain that if you were to be with him during the next very trying months you would be his salvation. However," he sighed, "as that cannot be we must hope he overcomes his bitter disappointment and manages to reach a sensible conclusion."

Before she went home Fleur was allowed into Alain's room. Sir Frank had assured her that he would not regain consciousness for some hours and that when he did so he would need very careful nursing and therefore no visitors would be admitted. Her eyes were drawn immediately to his face, etched darkly against the crisp smoothness of the pillows. His head was held firmly in position by supports placed on either side of it and his disturbing eyes were cloaked by a web of bandages. For once his long, sensitive fingers were at rest, no longer hovering over a sheathed rapier but resting lightly and unmoving against the white sheet—each finger outstretched as if, to her fevered imagination, out-thrust in pointing accusation.

She was present the morning Sir Frank chose to tell Alain the results of his findings. It was a week after the operation. Alain was no longer confined to bed but was sitting by the window, his jewel-colored dressing gown accentuating his postoperative pallor. Against all orders he had parted the curtains slightly so that delicate rays of the sunshine he loved so much played upon his raven-dark head and warmed his stern features with a honey-toned glint. With one irritable movement he conveyed his annoyance of the web of bandages still cloaking his eyes, and Fleur braced herself, when Sir Frank entered, for yet another rebellious argument that they should be removed.

Sir Frank, however, gave him no time to remonstrate. With a warning look toward Fleur, he strode up to Alain and delivered his own surprise attack with such hearty bonhomie that Fleur knew instinctively he was about to blunder.

"Well, Alain, I think it's time we had a little talk!"

Alain's nostrils flared with immediate antagonism. Fleur ached to tell him that nervous concern was the cause of Sir Frank's irritating tactics, but she was not given time to intervene.

"Indeed, yes." Alain's voice was tipped with steel. "By all means let us talk if doing so will mean an end to the playacting I have had to endure this past week!"

"Playacting?" Sir Frank was nonplussed.

Fleur was not entirely surprised when Alain's cold voice bit back, "Do you think me such a fool I can't tell the difference between success and failure? Even if I did not have physical signs to guide me, your own excessive sympathy and the anxiety in your voice would have been ample warning! Added to that, I've had Fleur's pitiful attempts to console me in secret. Obviously she, too, is aware that the operation was a failure, because every nuance in her voice is known to me and she has betrayed in a hundred different ways the heart-felt pity she is feeling!"

His savage resentment and acute perception rendered them both speechless. Hopelessly, with tear-filled eyes, Fleur appealed to Sir Frank, and when he gave a shrug of failure her breath caught in a half-strangled sob. Again, Alain demonstrated his amazing sensitivity by catching the barely audible sound and swinging savagely toward her.

"Don't shed tears for me. I will not tolerate pity! From now on I must resign myself to the life of a blind man—I must learn to read braille and walk with a white stick. I must also learn to tolerate pity and to accept expressions of sympathy from others, but not from you, Fleur—never from you! Always you must be honest with me, do you hear? If I were ever to discover that you had lied to me, that would be the day I should give up completely!"

Fleur found her voice. "I wouldn't lie to

you, Alain, and you must believe what I tell you now. Your case isn't hopeless! Sir Frank was trying to tell you that in another few months he'll be able to conclude the operation successfully. Only a small area of infection needs to be treated and after that all will be plain sailing. Please, Alain, listen to him, I beg of you!"

His answer was to reach up with a curse to pull the offending bandages from his eyes. He threw them to the floor, then lifted his head high. "Let that be the end of it!" he decreed with finality, his bitter disappointment blinding him to reason. "I never wish to hear another word on the subject!"

DURING THE WEEKS that followed, Sir Frank and Fleur disregarded that wish many times, but Alain remained adamantly opposed to any future operation. Finally, as he grew stronger and the time for his departure grew nearer, they had to concede defeat, although Fleur secretly cherished the hope that he might change his mind once he was back in his own surroundings; that the urge to see what he could now only sense would escalate within him. So, even though the outings they had had before his operation had recommenced and she was in his company almost every day, she gradually ceased to speak of it, because she had no wish to be hurt by the inward anger that seemed to be increasing as gradually as his returning strength.

During his convalescence he had become a frequent visitor to her home. He was now a firm favorite with her parents and he in return seemed to find pleasure and relaxation in their undemanding company. It was during one of these visits as they sat together in the garden soaking in the tranquillity of its solitude, that he astounded her by asking casually, "Fleur, will you marry me?"

He was lounging in a garden chair, negligently chewing a stalk of grass, when he tossed the startling question across to her, and although he must have sensed her amazed reaction he gave no sign of it.

"Wh—what did you say?" she whispered, afraid to repeat his question in case she had imagined it.

Impatiently he sat up and threw away the piece of grass. "I need you, Fleur. I can't face the thought of going back to France without you. Will you at least think about it?"

Her heartbeats quickened so much she felt the vibrations right through her body. She loved him so much she would happily have died for him, and yet he had sounded almost indifferent when he asked her to become his wife. Her lips parted, eager to tell him how much she loved him, but before the first happy words could escape he turned her heart to stone by continuing calmly, "It would be a marriage of convenience, of course. I would expect nothing more of you than I have received these past weeks; you have become my eyes—through you I am able to see again. I promise you—" he seemed presumptuously certain he would not be refused "—that you, too, will benefit from the alliance."

When the slow, hot tide of humiliation receded, she felt a gladness—a desperate shamed gladness—that he could not see the effect his words had had upon her. His cold, clinical offer of marriage was the greatest hurt she had ever suffered, and her only comfort lay in the fact that he was completely unaware of the feelings she had for him. He had not moved, but sat with his head inclined slightly, in a listening attitude, trying to gauge her reaction, so she remained perfectly still until her mind was calm and her trembling body was controlled.

Sharply he questioned, "Are you still there?"

The words underlined his need of her, a need far greater than he would admit, and her gentle heart flooded with compassion as it ignored his arbitrary demands and heeded only his subconscious cry for help.

"Yes, I'm here," she answered, completely intent upon making her voice sound calm and unruffled.

He relaxed, a slight smile curving his lips. "Good, I was afraid you hadn't heard. Well, what is your answer, Fleur? Will you marry me and return with me to France?"

"Yes." Her voice was a mere thread of sound, but he heard it and his smile widened, taking on a hint of cynicism.

"Thank you, I thought the idea would appeal to you."

She had to strive hard to retain her composure, to remember how hurt and alone he was and, deep down, how very much afraid. For two years he had lived in hope; now all hope was gone and to face the future he needed to have an anchor, someone who understood all his needs but who would make no claim upon his dead emotions. She remembered Sir Frank's words: "I'm certain that if you were to be with him during the next very trying months you would be his salvation!" Perhaps she was being self-sacrificial, even criminally foolish, in allowing herself to be used in such a way, but he had asked, and loving him she could refuse him nothing.

He was, he thought, under no illusions as to her motives. With one cynical black eyebrow raised, he drawled, "You like the idea of becoming a *comtesse*?"

She looked blankly back at him, then remembering he could not see, she stammered foolishly, "C-comtesse?"

"Oh, come now." He laughed unpleasantly. "Don't pretend you didn't know that as my wife you will become the Comtesse de Treville? My mother will then become the dowager Comtesse, and a very great relief it will be to her to hand over her duties. According to sentiments she has expressed often in the past, she is tired of organizing things at the château and your arrival will allow her more time for leisure."

Fleur's bewilderment was complete. "I simply don't understand you, Alain!" She appealed for an explanation. "Are you telling me that you are the Comte de Treville and that you own a château? If that is so, then I could never accept your proposal—the very idea of becoming a comtesse terrifies me! Please say it's all a joke. . . ."

"It's no joke, I assure you." He stiffened

with pride. "Our title is one of the oldest in France and the Château des Fleurs was built by my ancestors in the twelfth century."

She was appalled. "But why didn't you tell me this before?" she gasped.

There was a small silence before he answered dryly, "I thought you knew. It was no secret at the hospital. There were times—" he frowned at the memory "—when some of the nurses forgot themselves far enough to call me the 'impossible Count,' among other things," he concluded.

Vaguely Fleur recollected a similar reference Jennifer had made. At that time she had thought it a nickname bestowed upon him by the nursing staff because of his arrogant manner, but now, too late, she realized the truth: he really was a count!

"Your father, also, was not unaware of the fact," he continued pointedly. "I told him myself days ago when I decided to ask you to become my wife. It would not have been *comme il faut* to have left your parents in any doubt of my ability to look after you."

"Oh, Alain!" She had to smile at this piece of old-world courtesy, charming though it was. Although her life had been very sheltered she was modern enough to appreciate that such practice had long fallen into disuse, and besides that, her father placed so little importance upon material things that he would never think to dwell upon that aspect of what Alain had told him. The knowledge he would seek from the man who wanted to marry his daughter would be whether or not she was loved, and Fleur doubted very much if the answer he would have received to that question would have left him satisfied.

Exercising his uncanny gift of knowing exactly what she was feeling, he sensed her bewilderment and attempted to divert her mind into different channels.

"Come, enough of this. You have accepted my proposal and I will not allow you to go back on your word. We must tell your parents what we have decided, then begin making arrangements for our wedding. I intend that it shall take place here, in England, so that I can present you at the Château des Fleurs as my wife—the new Comtesse de Treville!"

This was decreed with such grim satisfaction that Fleur was immediately suspicious. With deep unease, she saw that he was smiling to himself, not a pleasant smile, rather the gloating, anticipatory smile of a man who has discovered a way to settle old scores. What little comfort she had found in the assumption that he had asked her to marry him because he needed her disappeared in an onrush of doubt. Who was waiting at the Château des Fleurs to receive the revenge Alain was planning? And why should it be necessary for him to take such a drastic step to secure such revenge? Her blood ran cold at the idea of being used as a weapon of spite. She loved Alain and however much she might deplore it she would always love him, but she was not blind to his faults. Bitter, intolerant, arrogantly immune to emotion. It was because he was all of these things that she did not refuse his proposal. Alain, Comte de Treville, was set on a crash course, heading for self-destruction, and she knew she could never desert him while there was even the faintest chance she might be able to help save him.

Chapter Four

THREE WEEKS LATER they were married in the small village church in which Fleur had been christened and which had since been the pivot of her existence. There was no long white dress, no fragrant bouquet, no virginal white veil to billow out behind her as she walked up the aisle toward her father, who was to conduct the service, and the dark-browed, complex man who was to be her husband. She wore a simple white suit with a matching hat and carried a small ivory-backed prayer book, but as she walked down the narrow aisle she noticed that the church was decorated with vase upon vase of sweet-smelling flowers, their colors splashing against the somber oak-paneled walls. She had to smile as she recognized her mother's touch; this was her only act of unspoken rebellion against Alain's express wish that there should be no fuss. Firmly, he had quelled all her mother's enthusiastic plans to invite half the district to the ceremony, to rehearse the choir in specially chosen hymns, to engage a caterer from the nearby town. He had even managed to charm her into accepting that it was unnecessary for her daughter to wear a full bridal outfit when her future husband was unable to see. Fleur was deeply grateful to her parents for their unquestioning cooperation and for the way they had striven to hide their deep misgivings and fear for the future of their only child.

She made very little sound as she moved down the aisle on Sir Frank's arm, but she knew by the way Alain's head went up that he had heard her. He moved forward, seemingly completely at ease, and held out his hand. Any onlooker would have been amazed by his sureness of touch and calm command of all his actions, but the slight twitching of a nerve at the corner of his mouth betrayed to Fleur the agony of frustration he felt at his own limitations and she was not sorry she had foregone the customary ceremony in order to save him from a much more prolonged ordeal.

It was a short, simple service, and afterward they went back to the vicarage for a meal. Jennifer, who together with Sir Frank had acted as witness, was the only one in high spirits, and her excited chatter carried them through what could have been a very subdued gathering. Although Alain was on edge, he managed to be charming to everyone, but when the time came for them both to leave for the airport he leaned his head back against the seat of the car Sir Frank had obligingly put at their disposal and muttered thankfully, "*Mon Dieu,* I'm glad that is over, I could not have endured another minute!"

Fleur did not reply. Alone for the first time with the man whom only a few hours earlier she had promised to love, honor and obey, she felt a stirring of blind panic.

The heavy gold band that weighted her finger was a fetter binding her to him for a lifetime; in her desperation she could have torn it from her finger and flung it out of the window!

Perhaps the reason he began to chat so calmly was because he sensed her panic—his perception of her moods was her greatest wonder. "Not long now until we are on our way to France," he told her with unusual kindness. "I think you will enjoy the flight. Did I remember to tell you we are going by an executive jet?"

She could only shake her head, but he carried on, "When I telephoned my mother to tell her we would arrive home whenever flight times made it possible she told me of an offer our neighbors had made to put their plane at my disposal whenever I needed it."

"Your neighbors have their own plane?" she asked, not really interested but glad of any diversion to take her mind off present problems.

He laughed. "Ah yes, but they are champagne people. They have a château near ours that they occupy only a few months in the year. They have built an airstrip on their grounds so that they can reach the château in as short a time as possible, but the plane is really for business use and Monsieur Chesnaye, whose plane it is, finds it invaluable for business trips, so it is not such a luxury as you might imagine."

"I see," Fleur faltered, her mind boggling at the notion of owning a private jet. "How convenient for him." Alain lapsed into silence at her seeming sarcasm, his brooding look once more predominant, and made no effort to entertain her.

A couple of hours later Fleur had her first taste of luxury. Sir Frank's chauffeur, who had been well instructed, saw them through the airport formalities, then handed them over to a young Frenchman who, he informed them, was the pilot of their plane. As he led the way across the tarmac Fleur could hardly believe the sleek, champagne-colored aircraft could possibly be the property of just one man. Discreetly, a smart young hostess guided Alain toward the steps that had been lowered for the ascent, then she ushered them both into the cabin, the interior of which was incredibly opulent.

There was seating for eight people: soft padded chairs with headrests in pale green leather resting on a champagne-colored carpet that flowed across the floor. Alain dropped into one of the seats with a sigh of relief and said to the hostess, "As soon as we are airborne fetch me a drink."

"*Certainement, monsieur,*" she replied. "And what about madame, would she like something?"

Madame! A shock of surprise kept Fleur silent as she assimilated the word, realizing for the first time how irretrievably far she had stepped into Alain's life. It was not the patiently waiting hostess who jolted her out of her preoccupation but Alain. His sharp, querying voice broke the silence with an insistence that called for a swift reply.

"Fleur! Why don't you answer?" It was the hidden call for reassurance of her presence that never failed to touch her and she answered from the heart.

"I'm here beside you, Alain, where I'll always be."

The eyes behind the dark glasses were unreadable, but when he sat back in his seat she saw a slow smile curl his lips and at the sight of it the panic in her heart subsided.

As she, too, relaxed in her seat, anxiety gave way to dawning excitement. This was her first flight, her first glimpse of a new world that seemed full of enchanting promise. All during the flight her eyes were fixed firmly upon the round window through which she watched England's coastline disappear gradually from sight until they were left suspended between motionless sky and heaving ocean. Disappointingly, because she was so looking forward to her first glimpse of France, thickening cloud began to obscure her view and for a long while she saw nothing of what lay beneath the speeding plane.

When the young hostess served them a delicious meal she told Fleur, whose enormous eyes and flushed cheeks were ample evidence that this was her first trip, that they were now over the Mediterranean coast and as the cloud was expected to lift she would soon have her first sight of the country's most beautiful scenery. Alain contributed nothing to the conversation, but sat in morose silence, eating hardly at all and barely tasting the champagne contained in the goblet he was twisting restlessly between his long sensitive fingers. Each mile they traveled he became more and more tense until, when the pilot's voice announced over the intercom, "We are now preparing to land, *Monsieur le Comte*," his grip tightened with such tensile strength around the stem of the goblet it shattered in his hand.

"Alain! Have you cut yourself?" Fleur leaned across to see for herself what damage had been done, but he swiftly dropped the offending glass and pushed his clenched fist deep into his pocket.

"It is nothing," he bit out, his face bloodless but with sweat beading his brow. "Please don't fuss!" She had no time to argue before the young hostess arrived to make sure their safety belts were fastened correctly, but her heart zoomed as swiftly low as the plane that was taking them so rapidly down to earth.

Her depression was so complete that she took little notice of the grand mansion in whose grounds the plane landed. She saw its tall superstructure in the distance and thought vaguely that the owners must surely be people of substance, but then she and Alain were being helped into the back of a sumptuous limousine and driven swiftly through an unfamiliar and unbelievably beautiful landscape such as she had previously seen only in technicolor movies. Even then, she had been hardly able to digest it.

To her left were mountains, far away but visibly snow-capped, and to her right blue sea flashed quickly into vision, then was as swiftly gone. The road wound through hills covered with thyme, rosemary, marjoram and broom, doubly attractive in their wild, uncultivated state. Small houses were sunk up to their roofs in pinewoods, and interesting little streams meandered down into valleys lush with semi-tropical vegetation.

And the smell! The overall sweetness of individual scents blending harmoniously together created a symphony of fragrance mere mortals could never hope to record nor manufacture. It was an Eden—a place where a chance breeze rippling restlessly through the aromatic petals could transport one unexpectedly into paradise. Every now and again they passed handsome, unobtrusive villas standing well back in spacious gardens filled with exotic flowers and sheltering palm trees, and all around tall cypress trees stood straight as sentinels against the hot blue sky.

She longed to exclaim with wonder as each fresh aspect of beauty came into view, but Alain's frowning countenance discouraged such exuberance, so she sat silent, her hands clasped tightly in her lap, absorbing it all in solitary wonder.

When the car slowed to turn into a drive flanked by massive stone pillars supporting huge wrought-iron gates, she was jolted into reality with a suddenness that caused her heart to spiral with alarm. Could this possibly be Alain's home? The towering edifice she saw in the distance reminded her of a feudal castle. Centuries of time had mellowed its thick stone walls to a warm shade of honey, but this in no way detracted from its grandeur. The rectangular, central part of the château was flanked by four corner towers connected by a sentry walk, and in her bemused state she would not have been surprised to see uniformed guardsmen ready to present arms or to hear a ten-gun salute booming from the battlements. As they drew nearer she saw a crowd of people grouped in the main court-yard and, incredibly, the last few yards of driveway were flanked by men each holding a French horn. Even as she watched, the car was sighted and, as if at a given signal, the men raised the horns to their lips and blew a triumphant blast to welcome their Comte and his new bride.

It was all so overwhelmingly feudal that Fleur felt she had been transported back into the twelfth century. No need to wonder now at the out-of-date attitudes of Alain; his unconscious arrogance and proud refusal to have his word questioned did not stem from conceit. They were the outcome of his upbringing and came as naturally to him as breathing. Here, deep in the heart of Provence, the French aristocracy were still revered and respected masters of all they surveyed.

The sound of the horns brought Alain erect, his jaw tightening as he battled for control before facing the coming ordeal. He had not been home for two years. All the time he had been in the hospital he had vowed never to return until he had regained his sight, but now that vow had had to be broken. Fleur's heart ached with pity for him, but she had been too much hurt in the past to risk communicating her feelings, so she subdued her own trepidation and spoke calmly.

"What a welcome, Alain! It must be very gratifying to know so many people are anxious to have you home again." She spotted a group of people standing a little apart at the top of the flight of stone steps leading to the château's main entrance. "I think I see your mother waiting, too. How excited she looks!"

"Who is with her?" When he grated out the question her eyes flew back to the group. Beside the slender figure of an old lady stood a young girl and a step or two behind her was a slim man who looked a few years younger than Alain. She was just about to pass on this information when the car slid quietly to a standstill and the chauffeur jumped down to help them out.

A full-throated roar of approval rose from the waiting crowd as she and Alain stepped from the car. Unobtrusively, she slipped her hand under his arm to guide him toward the house and to her surprise he accepted the gesture without a frown, willing for once to put up with interference rather than humble himself by stumbling in front of the watching eyes.

Chattering like excited birds the crowd surged forward, women and girls dressed in black with kerchiefs protecting their heads from the sun; small boys, brown-limbed and cheeky-faced, holding onto their fathers' hands; and older men with their berets doffed in respectful homage to the young *Comte* they obviously all adored.

The first genuinely happy smile Fleur had ever seen from him creased Alain's face as he returned their greetings, answering by name the owner of each voice as if he were able to see and recognize all those who spoke to him. One very old lady pushed her way to the front of the crowd and grabbed hold of his sleeve as he passed. With tears streaming down her wrinkled brown face she clung to him and sobbed, *"Ah, mon pauvre petit Alain, si pitoyable!"*

Fleur's French was rusty, but the sentiment was unmistakable and she blanched inwardly, waiting for a storm to break over the old woman's head. But Alain reached out to find the old woman's hand and when it was clasped tightly in his own he answered gently, *"Merci, Maman Rouge, pour votre sympathie,"* before disengaging himself and walking swiftly on.

Fleur was choking back unshed tears when they reached the bottom of the steps where his family was gathered. Luckily, before she needed to instruct him on the ascent, the solitary man detached himself from the family group and bounded down the steps to give assistance.

"Welcome home, Alain, you have been far too long away!" he greeted him as he grasped his elbow to guide him up the stairs.

The smile faded from Alain's lips at the sound of his voice and his astringent answer left no one in any doubt of his displeasure. "One would hardly expect the mouse to rejoice at the absence of the cat, Louis. Can it be that you welcome the curtailment of your pleasure, or are you perhaps hoping that my wits have been dulled as well as my sight?"

Fleur gasped, and the young man reddened under his tan. "Come now, Alain, is that the way to return a cousin's greeting?" He bowed to Fleur, missing nothing of her wide-eyed distress and the droop of her soft, vulnerable mouth. He frowned for a second, then with a very Gallic shrug he shed his discomfiture and twinkled, "Your wife is looking quite shocked, Alain. Please reassure her that I am not such a villain as your words suggest, for I swear she is ready to take flight!"

Alain's frown deepened and his tone was dry when he introduced her. "Fleur, this is my cousin Louis. If you are wise you will disregard every word he says, because although he is in some ways harmless—without malice, temper or sense—he has no scruples whatsoever about idling away his time and then lying to the teeth to defend his actions," he finished contemptuously.

Fleur's sympathetic eyes met those of the unrepentant Louis, but she looked quickly away after a brief nod, too embarrassed to return his impish smile. It was a relief when they reached the top of the steps and Alain's mother. She was standing quite still, watching with painful intensity each step he took, silently urging him not to stumble as he made his way toward her. Fleur was sure that if it had not been for the watching crowd she would have discarded the dignity she wore with the air of a queen and rushed to enfold him in her arms, but as it was she restrained her natural impulses and behaved in the way expected of the dowager Comtesse. Fleur suffered a chill of fear at the thought of this same aristocratic behaviour being expected of her: she knew she was totally incapable of shouldering such a demanding burden. She dared not think what the immaculately dressed and coiffured old lady was thinking of her own unsophisticated manner and indifferent dress. Clothes interested her because she liked nice things, but there had never been sufficient money at the vicarage to allow her to indulge in luxuries and she had seen so much of other people's miseries, brought about through lack of money; she had considered herself fortunate in having enough to fulfill her everyday needs.

"My dear, dear boy!" As his mother moved toward him Alain reached out to enfold her slight figure in his arms and for a moment they stood close together in silent communication. After a few moving seconds he put her away from him and turned his head in search of Fleur. "Maman," he said when Fleur reacted instantly to his gesture by moving to his side and slipping her cold hand into his, "you must be anxious to meet your daughter-in-law." Then, opposing Fleur's shyness by drawing her farther forward, he said simply, "Fleur, this is my mother. I hope you'll come to love her as much as I do."

The moment was poignant with feeling, but even so through her rioting senses Fleur heard the sharp angry gasp that came from the girl waiting to welcome Alain. It was evident that he had heard it, too, when his easy assurance dropped from him like a cloak and he swung around toward the sound with a sharp intake of breath, his dark glasses hiding whatever message was betrayed in his eyes.

Fleur could never afterward remember what

she said to his mother, or what his mother said in return. She knew she was welcomed warmly, with tender tearfulness, and she registered the fact that the old Comtesse would be easy to love, but her whole being was centered upon the meeting between Alain and the girl whose unspoken presence had had such an uncanny effect upon him. Her beauty was so incredibly perfect that Fleur blinked. She was as dark-haired as Alain, but her skin was the soft matt whiteness of a magnolia blossom. Brilliant red lipstick colored velvet-soft pouting lips so that the eye was immediately drawn to admire their faultless outline, and her petite, voluptuously rounded figure was dressed to perfection in a white dress so superior in style and cut it loudly proclaimed itself a product of one of the most exclusive fashion houses of Paris. She stared at Alain, not bothering to hide her angry dismay at the news she had obviously heard for the first time from his own lips, and as the silence lengthened her large brown eyes clouded with temper and mortification.

"Is that Célèstine?" Fleur went rigid when she recognized sharp malice in Alain's voice, sensing that one of the many questions seething in her brain was about to be answered. She was even more convinced of it when he continued to speak with cruel pleasure. "Célèstine, I would like to introduce you to my wife—the new Comtesse de Treville!"

This, then, was the moment for which Alain had been waiting! For some reason this girl was the instigator of his determined, cold-blooded thirst for revenge!

Chapter Five

FLEUR STOOD CONTEMPLATING an enormous built-in closet that spanned the width of one bedroom wall. She had just hung up the last of her dresses, but even though she had spaced them out as much as possible the great empty void that remained emphasized the sparsity of her belongings. She shrugged and closed the door, determining at the same time to shut from her mind the worrying thoughts that clamored for admittance: thoughts about her own simple background and her inability to cope with the totally unexpected magnificence now surrounding her; thoughts about Alain's disturbing family, his friendly, aristocratic mother, his charmingly inconsequential cousin and lastly his friend, the beautiful Célèstine Chesnaye who had made a tremendous effort to overcome her chagrin when she was introduced to the new Comtesse de Treville, but whose brilliant, angry eyes had belied the courteous words she had been forced to utter.

Fleur shivered at the memory. They were all to dine together that evening, and although she had welcomed the Comtesse's suggestion that she might like to rest before dinner, she knew her too active mind would not allow her to do so. She wandered across yards of rose-patterned carpet toward the window, turning her back upon the sumptuous furnishings, endeavoring to recover her sense of proportion by gazing out upon the simplicity of nature. But outside, as within, the outlook was so lavish that she felt satiated, and a longing for home and for the sight of a cool English meadow overwhelmed her. Two crystal tears were on the brink of falling when a gentle knock sounded on the door. Hastily, she wiped her hand across her eyes before calling out: "*Entrez!*"

She was expecting a maid to appear and was disconcerted when the door opened to admit the tiny regal figure of Alain's mother.

"Comtesse! I didn't realize it was you." She

blushed like a schoolgirl caught out in some misdemeanor, then in a nervous rush she remembered her manners. "Please—" she pulled forward a chair "—won't you sit down?"

The Comtesse smiled graciously and accepted the proffered chair. Sitting straight-backed, in a gray lace gown with gems sparkling from a brooch pinned to her chest and from numerous rings upon her fingers, she epitomized the luxury that had already begun to infect Fleur with a sense of inferiority—causing her nervousness to increase.

"Sit down, child," the Comtesse demanded kindly. "We have many things to discuss. I am fully aware of the strain you are undergoing, and, knowing such a strain would prevent you from sleeping, I thought this a propitious time for us to talk. Do you mind, my dear, or would you rather I left you to rest?"

"Oh, no," Fleur assured her earnestly, eager to get to know her better, "you are most welcome, Comtesse!"

"Then to start with—" she leaned forward to pat her hand "—we shall have to agree upon what you are to call me. You are the Comtesse de Treville now, and must be addressed as such, whereas I am now the dowager

Comtesse." She seemed not one whit disturbed by this fact, but seemed to hesitate before voicing her next request. "If the idea does not offend you, my dear, I would like you to call me Maman as Alain does. . . ."

Fleur's eyes widened with surprise, not at the request, but at the diffidence in the old lady's voice.

She was shy! The regal old aristocrat was as afraid as any other new mother-in-law might be that she would be rebuffed. Fleur slid from her chair to kneel at her feet. Fighting tears of loneliness, she looked up into her face and told her simply, "How nice of you, Maman, to do me such an honor."

For a moment the Comtesse looked as if she were about to break down, but her shaking mouth was pulled sternly into order when years of self-discipline came to her aid.

"You know," she said shakily, "I find many pleasing omens surrounding your arrival here as Alain's bride. For instance, has it not occurred to you how appropriately you are named?"

Fleur caught her meaning. "Because my name is Fleur and this is the Château des Fleurs?" She smiled. "Yes, it certainly is an odd coincidence."

"And also—" the Comtesse's hands were shaking "—today it is two years exactly since Alain's accident. How very upsetting my dear boy would have found his homecoming if he had not had you by his side to comfort him."

Fleur's smile faded. Alain truly was a solitary man.; It hurt to discover how little he allowed her to know about himself, how thoroughly he excluded her from sharing his troubles. There was no doubt in her mind now that he intended she should remain ignorant of all past events, but there were questions she had to have answered if she was not to be thought unfeeling by his family and friends who would expect her to be informed of all the facts.

"How . . . how did the accident happen, Maman?" she forced herself to ask.

The Comtesse flinched, but Fleur's anxious expression, the pain darkening her blue eyes to violet, showed plainly that the answer to the question was important to her, and so, slowly mastering her distress, the woman answered, "No one knows to this day what really happened. Alain was working at the distillery, experimenting with some new fragrance he had evolved and had become quite excited about." She checked before continuing to make sure

Fleur understood; then, when she saw her look of bewilderment, she elaborated, "Our family has been in the perfume business for centuries, my dear. Surely you've heard of Maison Treville perfumes, our trade name?"

Fleur remembered a tiny vial of the extravagantly expensive perfume she had received as a Christmas present from Jennifer one year. She had treasured it to the last drop and even afterward the empty bottle had lain in a drawer so that the last whiff of scent could add fragrance to her handkerchiefs. "But of course," she agreed, "everyone has heard of Maison Treville!"

The Comtesse gave a pleased nod. "We are well known but not, I think, without just cause. Alain is an expert on perfumes—he has had years of training and a lifetime of familiarity with the industry, of course, but then so has Louis and he is not half so good at his job. Alain has something extra, an abnormally keen sense of smell that enables him to detect the finest shade of odors and to identify every ingredient used to make the particular perfume he is creating. But his real art and skill lies in his ability to blend various scents and essences to produce new and exciting perfumes, so perfectly balanced and combined that even the greatest expert—and we have many among our neighbors—find it very difficult to detect the ingredients of which they are composed. Yes," she sighed, "the industry has certainly missed Alain these past two years. Louis, I'm afraid, simply does not have that extra bit of magic that is the mark of genius. Not that he does not try—" she was quick to defend her own note of censure "—it is simply that he is still a boy at heart and would much rather seek his pleasures outside of the business. Once," she said as if to herself, "Alain, too, was as carefree. . . ." She broke off, shook herself free of some unhappy memory and then continued firmly, "You must let Louis take you around the works, Fleur. I'm sure you will be fascinated; he can be a most entertaining companion."

"I'm sure of that, Maman," Fleur agreed, reluctant to be forced into Louis's company in case she should incur Alain's displeasure, but unable to find sufficient excuse to refuse. "Perhaps some day."

"Nonsense!" The Comtesse seemed determined. "You shall go tomorrow, I'll arrange it with Louis myself."

Gently Fleur reminded her, "You were about to tell me about Alain's accident." But the Comtesse was either too tired or she found the subject too painful. With a small shrug she dismissed it. "There is very little to add. One of the workmen rushed up to the château with the news that Alain's eyes had been splashed with acid while he worked in his laboratory—the acid is used to clear the utensils of all smell so that future experiments are not ruined by contamination from a previous one. Even Célèstine, who was with him at the time, can give us no clear idea of what happened, and as for Alain—he has always refused to speak of it."

Fleur's warning hackles rose at these last words, but before she could question her further the Comtesse stood up to make her departure.

"We will talk again soon," she told her fondly, "but now I must go if I am not to be overtired before evening." She turned to walk toward the door, then hesitated. "Fleur, *ma petite*, I really came to tell you how very pleased I am that you accepted Alain. Life for you might become difficult—he can be very trying at times—but please never have any doubts that you have done the right thing. However unkind he might be, however hurtful or secretive, there is no doubt that you are essential to his happiness—and he to yours. Please accept a mother's blessing and gratitude."

Long after she had left Fleur pondered upon her words. Without being disloyal, she had managed to convey her sympathy and the bewilderment she felt at the change in her son. Fleur did not find it hard to believe Alain had once been a devil-may-care boy who could have caused his mother some anxious moments. Had she not recognized at first sight of him the cavalier streak that ran through his blood, the swashbuckling, debonair attitude that to a woman meant excitement, racing pulses and a dangerous attraction? She put her hand to her throat where a pulse was throbbing rapidly. Alain could be like that again, she was certain, if only he could rid himself of the black depression that bedeviled him, but if he did, would he look to her, the simple daughter of a country parson, to share his excitement or would his thoughts be more likely to turn toward Célèstine, who would make a fitting mate for his tempestuous nature?

Suddenly she felt suffocatingly hot. She decided she needed a cooling shower before going downstairs for dinner.

Alain and she were sharing a suite; she was in the main bedroom and he was in a smaller room with a connecting bathroom that they were obviously meant to share. There was no sound from his room as she turned on the tap and stepped under the glass-enclosed shower to enjoy the sensation of needle-sharp jets of water splashing against her skin. It was so invigorating that she prolonged her enjoyment of it until she began to feel numb with cold. Then, rather than turn on the hot tap, she groped for a towel and began to rub herself vigorously to get rid of the chill. She was so engrossed that she failed to hear the door open and was only aware of Alain's presence when she looked up and saw him dressed in a bath-robe, walking slowly forward in the direction of the shower. Her hand flew to her mouth to smother a gasp, but she was not quick enough and his head jerked upright when he heard the small sound.

"Who's there?" he jerked out.

She could not answer, searing embarrassment rendering her dumb so that even though she knew he could not see her she was incapable of replying.

"Answer me, damn you!" He made an angry move forward, but caught his shin on a

stray stool and would have overbalanced if she
had not instinctively run forward to catch him.
He caught hold of her shoulder and with one
inflammatory touch made her vividly aware
that she was no longer a girl, a shy dreamer,
but a woman with a husband whose touch was
fire.

"Fleur!" He spoke her name in a low hiss
and for a moment seemed ready to push her
angrily away.

"I'm sorry, Alain," she stuttered, crimson
with distress and trying terribly hard to
remember that the dark eyes blazing down at
her really could not see. "I tried, but I couldn't
turn the key in your lock. I think it must be
jammed. . . ."

When she became conscious of his sudden
stillness her voice trailed into silence. He still
held her, and gradually, almost imperceptibly,
his grasp was tightening. In his eyes, no longer
hidden by dark glasses, a tiny flame was
kindling deep, deep down, and his mouth had
broken from its grim lines to pucker at the
corners with the beginning of a vagrant smile.
Slowly he drew her forward until his breath
was fanning the damp strands of hair at her
temples, curling them into fine baby tendrils.
His voice, whimsically teasing, was startling,

coming as it did from a man who was a stranger to tenderness.

"Louis tells me you are beautiful, a lovely English rose was his description. . . ." She trembled under his touch, his closeness rendering her incapable of response. "Do you mind if I find out for myself?" his tormenting continued. "I'm at a decided disadvantage in being unable to picture a wife whose beauty, according to Louis, will make me the envy of my friends!"

She did not flinch when his hands reached out to touch her face. Lightly, his fingers traced across her smooth brow and hesitated momentarily against her wide sweep of eyelashes before continuing down the contours of her cheeks.

"Candid blue eyes as large and soft as purple pansies," he murmured, repeating Louis's description. "Hair so heavy with gold dust that specks have fallen to gild the tips of thick dark lashes. And lips—" his fingertips scorched her mouth "—miniature petals of pink velvet."

She struggled with mixed feelings of alarm and restless excitement. Blood was pounding in her ears, his touch leaving her inflamed and full of strange yearnings that accelerated when his searching hands swept down the slim column of her neck and lingered deliberately upon the smooth skin of her shoulders. Overcome with feeling, the towel she was holding slipped from her nerveless hands to the floor and at the same moment he betrayed, with a sharp intake of breath, that his breaking point had been reached. He pulled her forward against him with hard strength and his lips sought hers in a long, brutal kiss that contained all the frustration built up inside him during two long years of abstinence. She responded with all her loving heart to the need she sensed within him, but even through the sensation of drowning that chased all misgivings to the four winds, a tiny part of her knew she was being made a substitute for someone and that the longing he was demonstrating was not for her but for some shadowy person belonging to his past. But as the kiss progressed she was swept past the point of caring.

With all her heart and soul she loved him and the depth of her love was such she was willing to be satisfied with any small part of himself he might be inclined to offer.

Just when it seemed they would drown together in the depths of passion, he pushed her away. Breathing heavily and with his jaw tightly clamped, he jerked out, "I'm sorry, terribly sorry, that should never have happened!" His fists clenched and unclenched as he fought for control. "I can offer no excuse for my behavior," he exclaimed. "I'm no celibate, I like the company of women and for two years it has been denied me, but that in no way absolves me from blame. My actions were despicable! Fleur—" she was shocked to see how white his face had become "—will you please forgive me?"

"Don't be sorry, Alain." She moved to put her arms around him once more, but he fastened her wrists in a vicelike grip and refused to let go. "Alain!" Her cry held a world of bewilderment. "There's no need for you to apologize. After all, I am your wife!"

The coldness of his answer strangled every hope she had cherished. "I married you for a purpose, but not for that purpose! I need you beside me, but, *mon Dieu,* even I do not understand why!" He spat out the words as if confounded by his own illogicality. "I'm beginning to realize that I cheated you by allowing you to marry half a man, but at the time when I asked you I thought I was doing you a service."

"Doing me a service?" she queried, suddenly cold.

There was an uncomfortable silence, then, obviously laboring under acute embarrassment, he admitted, "I owe you complete honesty, you have always been honest with me and I must not do you less than justice in this respect."

She stiffened, realizing that she was about to hear something upsetting. Almost subconsciously she noted the way his hands were clasping and unclasping—a sure sign of unease—and that his hair, usually strictly controlled, was rioting over his head in unruly confusion as a result of her having run her fingers through its dark mass. She forced her mind back to what he was saying. It began almost like an awkward confession.

"For various reasons, one of which you already know, I needed a wife, and you seemed an ideal choice. When I proposed marriage I was under the impression that you were a *célibataire*—" she went rigid with surprise "—a middle-aged spinster stuck in the middle of nowhere, at the beck and call of her father and with no hope of ever escaping the rut she had been forced to occupy." He held up his hand for silence when his quick ears caught the sound of her incredulous gasp and continued grimly, "No one thought to mention that you were a young and lovely girl who could probably have had the choice of half a dozen men—not, that is, until Louis told me, and by then it was too late. I thought you owed your shyness and honesty to a strict upbringing. Had I known that youth was the major factor I would never have taken advantage of you as I did. To me, you were a good companion, an unassuming, undemanding person with whom I could be myself and with whom I never needed to act a part. Believe me, I was astonished and most upset when Louis described you to me. In fact, I thought he was playing out another of his stupid jokes, and that is the reason I acted as I did just now. I had to know!"

Her mouth was so stiff she could hardly manage to speak, but she finally managed a harsh, dry laugh before charging him, "If you really thought me a middle-aged spinster—no doubt with thick ankles and wearing tweeds—why did you want to marry me? Why?" she stressed bitterly.

Through a haze of tears she saw him shrug. "Call me a coward if you like, but all I wanted was someone to lean on—someone to protect me from the cloying sympathy I knew I could expect when I arrived here. I also needed eyes, eyes that could see and describe to me in detail what I need to know, and someone who, without prevarication, would speak the truth to me always. I wanted that, Fleur, and I still do, but I now realize that the luxury and the unlimited money, which are all I can offer in return, don't mean half so much to you as they would have to the person I thought you were." His forehead wrinkled into a puzzled frown. "I simply don't understand why you agreed to my proposal. What possible reason could you have had for tying yourself to a blind man?"

Her heart took a frightened leap. He must never know of the foolish dreams she had woven around his unsuspecting head. Better by far that he should suspect her of mercenary motives than that he should guess the extent of her foolishness. Fighting to subdue the traitorous bottom lip that was quivering so uncontrollably it would betray her terrible hurt, she answered stonily, "Perhaps you were not so very wrong in your judgment of me. Gillingham is a dead hole and I often longed to get away from it; I was hardly likely to ignore any offer of escape. So you've really no need to condemn yourself or your actions, Alain. You bought me, but I was willing to be bought, and only time will tell which one of us will get the better of the bargain. Let's leave it at that, shall we?"

His proud nostrils flared. He seemed so taken aback he could find no words to answer her flippancy. For a second he looked ready to protest, to point out the glaring flaws in her argument, but then his lips twisted into his usual mockery of a smile and the light faded from his eyes, leaving them dark with fathomless thoughts. Sketching a quick salute, he turned on his heel and left her, cold and shaking, to cry out her heart in the empty room.

Chapter Six

THERE IS A PEAK of suffering that, once reached, results in a blessed state of numbness. When Fleur had gone over each of Alain's brutal statements and forced herself ruthlessly to accept that she had meant so little to him that he had not stopped even to wonder about her looks or to consider her innermost feelings, she reached that peak and her resultant numbness carried her over what, in other circumstances, might have been a difficult evening.

After leaving the bathroom she had sat on the edge of her bed and willed herself to think things out, to decide upon a course of action that would do the least harm to everyone concerned.

She had rejected immediately the idea of returning home to England; she was determined that her parents should not be subjected to more worry on her account. The yearning to go, to pour out her troubles into their receptive ears, was almost overwhelming, but she was too concerned for their peace of mind ever to burden them with her troubles even though she knew she could count on their wholehearted support.

And the old Comtesse—she, too, must never learn the extent of the breach between her son and his new bride. Alain had been most emphatic on this point when the question of sharing a suite had arisen. He had apologized, but explained that his mother was so ecstatically happy about his marriage that he wanted no flaw to mar that happiness. She had agreed to his request that they put on an act whenever his mother was in their vicinity and so, for the Comtesse's sake, she must keep her word even if it meant remaining at the château indefinitely or, at least, for as long as Alain decreed that it was necessary. However hard she sought she could reach no other conclusion, and so the decision had been taken.

One thing she resolved, however, was that Alain would no longer find her subservient to his every whim, nor passively accepting his every brutal word without protest. She, too, had a life to live and, unpleasant though the future promised to be, he would not be allowed to make it unbearable.

She dressed for dinner and when she was ready made her way reluctantly downstairs to meet the challenge of her new environment. Once outside her room her steps faltered; the sheer size and magnificence of it all was frightening.

Wide-eyed, she took in the tremendous sweep of wood paneling that stretched high above her head until it reached a huge domed ceiling where cherubs with round cheeks and plump little bodies garlanded with flowers were painted so perfectly that she felt an impulse to reach up and cuddle them. Long slender windows let in the light, throwing into relief panels so richly and fancifully carved they could have been the work of a metal beater or silversmith, but in wood. Delicate statuary was positioned here and there in niches along the walls and ironwork as ethereal as a cobweb shawl supported the banister of a wide marble staircase that swept down to the great hall and merged into rose and white blocks of marble that made patterns of color on the floor. Numerous doors lined the walls of the hall, and seeing one slightly ajar, she hurried over to it, anxious to be rid of the feeling of awe that threatened to demoralize her completely. But once inside there was no respite from her fears.

The room she entered was a library in which thousands of colorful leather-bound books were ranged from floor to ceiling. Mobile steps to enable a searcher to reach the uppermost row beckoned enticingly and in another few seconds she might have succumbed to the temptation were it not for the voice that sounded startlingly close to her ear.

"Ah, *la belle* Fleur! How pleased I am that you decided to come down a little early. We can now proceed to become acquainted."

At the sight of her startled reaction Louis grinned apologetically.

"I'm sorry if I made you jump. Come, let me pour you a drink to make up for my lack of consideration."

She had to return his cheeky smile. However small an opinion Alain might have of him she could not resist the spontaneous charm of her new cousin.

"Thank you," she accepted, "that will be very nice."

He moved toward a table stocked with an assortment of bottles. "Will Pernod do?"

"Yes, anything," she replied, nervous of admitting that she had no idea to what she was being committed.

As he sauntered across with her drink he appraised her lazily. In her simple blue gown—painstakingly cut out and stitched together by herself and her mother—she represented an intriguing novelty to the blasé, sophisticated young man who for years had flirted mildly and often dangerously with most of the women contained within his circle of rich friends.

He was suddenly aware, as his glance lingered on her tremulous mouth and caught the nervous-fawn expression in her lovely eyes, how bored he had become by orchids and how much more interesting he might find the natural beauty of an English country flower. Hothouse plants, though delicately lovely, were inclined to wilt, but Fleur's fresh, natural appeal lacked neither character nor stamina.

She sipped her drink—its aniseed flavor was not much to her liking—and wondered when the rest of the family would appear. Louis's bold eyes were not disconcerting her half so much as he hoped, but she was on edge at the thought of another meeting with Célèstine, who she knew was to dine with them that evening.

With a perception as acute as Alain's, he drawled, "Célèstine will be busy making herself look as stunning as possible. She is not slow to recognize a challenge to her so far undisputed claim to being the district's greatest female attraction. Even though—" he breathed his next words into his glass as he tossed back his drink "—the object of her efforts is quite unable to appreciate them."

With a dignity that earned his quick respect, she looked him straight in the eyes and stated quietly, "You mean Alain, don't you? Why do you hint? If there is something I should know why don't you just tell me outright?"

He was taken aback by her honest simplicity and for a second he felt an uncharacteristic twinge of shame. But he quickly recovered and shrugged, a very Gallic shrug. "Everyone around here knows Alain and Célèstine were to have been married, so it's just as well that you, too, should know." He shifted uncomfortably when he saw her bite her lip, then hastened to assure her, "You need not feel

upset, it was all over two years ago. Célèstine
broke off the engagement shortly after Alain
had his accident. He was in the hospital at the
time and we all thought her action pretty
mean, in fact, I don't think Maman has
forgiven her even yet, but he never allows us to
guess his feelings and he would never afterward speak of Célèstine. That is why I was so
astonished by his actions today. We tried to
persuade her to leave before you and Alain
arrived, but she insisted upon staying to
welcome him. She thought, of course, that he
would be arriving alone because Maman, who,
as I've already stated, does not feel at all
disposed to be friendly, made me promise not
to mention a word to her about the wedding. I
think," he said, with a wicked smile, "spiteful
little puss that she is, she was enjoying the
prospect of seeing Célèstine's humiliation when
she heard the news."

Fleur did not return his smile. "Am I to
surmise then that she was intending to try to
make up her quarrel with Alain?"

His brow wrinkled. "No one ever quite
knows what Célèstine is intending. We have
seen very little of her here at the château
during the past two years. I suspect she may
have heard of the possible success of his last

operation, then laid her plans accordingly. She arrived here a week ago, full of helpful suggestions for getting Alain back home—it was she who arranged for her father's plane to fly him back, did you know?" When she nodded briefly he continued, "It must have been as great a shock to her as it was to us to learn of the failure of the operation. I can only hazard a guess that the reason she stayed on here today had its basis in curiosity, and the shock of seeing you and learning of your marriage must have made her resolve to stay on. Why, I cannot imagine, unless it is that she regards Alain as her own personal property and that, even though she herself would never countenance being tied to a blind man, she resents the fact that he is now your husband." He frowned, and concluded with uncharacteristic seriousness, "I should be very wary of her, if I were you, Fleur. She can be a dangerous enemy and, spoiled brat that she is, she won't hesitate to try to make you pay for any imaginary wrongs."

She blanched. Louis's words had created within her an ache that, added to the pain already inflicted by Alain, was threatening to break her gallant spirit completely. Louis had not spared her, but she did not blame him, because at last she had been made aware of the motive behind Alain's actions.

It was Célèstine he had wanted to hurt; she who had motivated the spite that had driven him into marriage with Fleur so that he could revenge the rejection he must have felt so deeply. She could have cried when she thought of the cruel blow Célèstine had dealt him, a blow that would have been hurtful at any time but which, coming at a time when he needed her most, must have been savage in its intensity.

She went so white that Louis became alarmed.

Cursing himself for his abruptness, he reached out to clutch her as she swayed and she was glad to rest against him for a second to marshal her swimming senses.

"Well, well!" As Célèstine appeared in the doorway with Alain a couple of paces behind her she voiced the words with malicious enjoyment.

"So you are up to your usual tricks, Louis! You have never been slow to make acquaintance with any reasonably good-looking woman, but this time you have excelled yourself. You would feel quite touched, Alain, if you could observe how well Fleur and Louis have taken to one another!"

Fleur's cheeks flamed as she jerked from the circle of Louis's arms. She had eyes only for Alain and her heart sank when she saw a great flood of anger darken his face. As he was standing in the semidarkness of the hall only she was acute enough to notice it, but when he advanced farther into the room he had composed his features into a mask of polite amusement.

"Tell me more, Célèstine," he said, his voice light. "I would be the most severely handicapped of husbands were it not for your ever ready vigilance on my behalf."

Fleur felt almost sorry for Célèstine. His words, teasingly light though they were, contained an allegation of spitefulness and were formed solely to inform her that he was aware of her baser motives. The smile faded from Célèstine's lips, leaving them a tight line of crimson anger, and Fleur shuddered as a chill feathered across her skin.

Louis was right, Célèstine would be a dangerous adversary, and if the look she had just aimed at them from across the room was any indication she had already declared war upon Louis and herself!

The Comtesse's arrival was a welcome relief.

When she entered the library they saw

immediately that her sharp instinct had
warned her something was wrong, and rather
than face almost certain inquisition they each
made an effort to disperse the pervading
atmosphere of disquiet. Surprisingly, because
her entry had been noiseless, Alain was the
first to greet her.

"Ah, *ma petite* Maman, so you have arrived
at last. Now, perhaps, we can eat."

Her troubled frown disappeared as she
responded to his teasing. "Tut, tut, Alain! As
usual you reprimand me for being late! But as
it is such a joy to have you back I shall forgive
you."

"How on earth did you know she was here,
Alain?" Célèstine was quite devoid of tact. "I
swear she made no sound!"

Fleur winced, but Alain smiled, quite
unperturbed.

"Have you forgotten already, Célèstine?"
When the Comtesse and Louis exchanged
smiles Fleur realized that she was the only one
who was puzzled.

"Of course not," she replied with a sulky
pout, "it had merely slipped my memory.
Your mother is wearing the perfume you devised exclusively for her and its fragrance obviously reached your senses seconds before her

actual presence. You always did enjoy playing that particular game, didn't you, Alain? It was your proud boast that even blindfolded you could tell immediately that your mother entered the room." Suddenly the pout disappeared, and her tone became intimate. "But have you forgotten, Alain, that you promised to create a perfume especially for me? Will it be the one you were working on when your accident happened, or has that formula been lost forever?"

Alain's face became so white that Fleur took an instinctive step toward him, but Louis's arm shot out to detain her and he shook his head, warning her not to interfere.

"More than a formula was lost that day," Alain bit out, his fists knotting as he strove to contain the feelings aroused by memory. "My loss of sight should be sufficient excuse to free me from that promise if, indeed, the promise was ever actually made!"

Unhampered by any feelings of sensitivity, Célèstine sidled up to plead with him. It was a pity, Fleur thought furiously, as she watched her pouting coquettishly up at him, he could not appreciate the pathos in her beautiful face nor the picture she made in her long, figure-molding gown of red silk jersey that contrasted so vividly with the muted background. She appeared as vibrantly alive as a slender-stemmed poppy. "But you must continue with your work, Alain," she urged him positively. "The delicate sense of smell that is your most valuable asset is unimpaired, and that, together with the knowledge you have gathered over the years, is the nucleus of your skill. All you lack is your sight, and I can help you there. You know you used to say I was a great help to you in the laboratory, and I could be again. You and I, Alain, could work together to bring back the magic that made Maison Treville so famous!"

"Are you implying that the magic has been lost?" the Comtesse intervened frostily, her black eyes snapping with anger.

Célèstine shrugged. "Maison Treville is resting upon its laurels and we all know it. Whatever you might be hoping to the contrary, dear Comtesse, you must admit that Alain's absence left a gap no one else was able to fill. There has not been one outstanding perfume created by the House during the past two years, and because of this your competitors are rubbing their hands with glee. The firm needs Alain's flair, his genius, because without it it cannot hope to retain its reputation of being the foremost in the industry."

Louis's face reddened, but he did not contradict Célèstine. Fleur felt terribly sorry for him as she glimpsed beneath his mask of nonchalant indifference the hurt of a boy who has endeavored to fill an older man's function only to fail miserably.

She was glad when Alain, who was now in full control of his emotions, took charge of the conversation.

"You seem very well informed, Célèstine, but I must ask you not to discuss affairs of business on my first night home. Louis and I have been constantly in touch during my absence and thanks to him there is nothing I do not know about the business."

Drawing himself upright, he pronounced distinctly, in a tone that implied he would brook no further argument, "As for your offer of help, it was most thoughtful of you to offer your assistance, but I hope you won't think me ungrateful if I decline to accept. I think you must have overlooked the fact that I now have a new partner, a permanent partner who will see me through all my difficulties—Fleur, my wife!"

The breath Célèstine drew sounded like a hiss. Her flamboyantly dressed figure was tensely erect as she weathered the snub he had so coolly administered, and Fleur felt a surge

101

of thankfulness that, for once, she was not on the receiving end of his caustic tongue. Alain smiled into the silence no one seemed willing to break.

Célèstine and he were the prominent actors, the stage was set for them alone and the rest of the cast seemed to be mere puppets placed there to give character to the scene. Fascinated, they watched the emotions that chased across Célèstine's proud, beautiful face: surprise, chagrin, rage, that came and went in quick succession, then finally, with the aid of tremendous effort, a sweet reasonableness that did not quite reach her eyes. She closed the gap between them and once more took hold of his sleeve. "You are quite right to chastise me, Alain," she sighed wistfully. "As usual I interfere in what is none of my business. Were my father here, he would confirm that it is one of my greatest failings, this affairs of business that he, too, insists are the affairs of men only. Forgive me, *mon ami?*"

Her charm was so electrifying that it would have broken through Fleur's mistrust were it not for the green danger signals she glimpsed when for a second her eyes met Célèstine's. They smoldered like those of a young, untamed mountain cat which, deprived of prey, is forced to harness its frustrations until the next killing. Such primitive emotion was alien to her nature and she quickly looked away.

Alain, however, seemed completely deceived.

His eyes alight with pleasure, he lifted her hand and kissed the tips of her fingers with a gallantry that would not have disgraced his cavalier ancestors. "Do not speak to me of forgiveness, *ma belle* Célèstine, when you know full well that between us is such deep understanding the word has become meaningless." He turned in the direction of the silent, waiting group and smiled, a boyish smile full of charm. "I think it's time we had dinner," he suggested, "so if you, Louis, will lead the way?"

Thankful at being released from their silent ordeal, Fleur, Louis and the Comtesse quickly obeyed, leaving Célèstine, purring with happiness, to follow on the arm of her suave adversary.

FLEUR WAS GRATEFUL to Louis for his attentiveness during the meal. Célèstine monopolized Alain's conversation, excluding everyone to the point of rudeness and he, surprisingly, seemed happy to allow her to do so. The Comtesse, however, was not, and as the meal progressed she made a determined effort to make the conversation general.

Making no attempt to hide her displeasure, she broke into a tale Célèstine was recounting to Alain concerning two friends unknown to his family.

"Alain, I have arranged for Louis to take Fleur around the distilleries tomorrow. She should enjoy the visit, don't you think?"

His head lifted, and the fork with which he had been toying with his food was laid carefully down upon his plate. "Why Louis?" he asked. "Is there some reason why I should not accompany her myself?" His tone was as cold as his mother's and she, sensitive to his every mood, flinched from his disapproval and became flustered.

Not for the world would she have put into words the obvious drawback his blindness would be in the role of a guide, but as he was so patiently waiting for an answer she searched for one.

"There is no reason why you should not go along, too, *mon fils*. Louis could then acquaint you with the changes that have been made during your absence and at the same time he could show Fleur around." With flags of distressed color high in her cheeks, she turned to Fleur and began feverishly to chatter. "First of all, they must take you to see the flower plantations, a sight so incredibly beautiful it must not be missed. You must also meet the pickers—some are local people, but most come as seasonal workers—among them families who have served us for generations. Many of them, such as Maman Rouge, for instance, were working here when I arrived as a bride, and their sons have grown up with Alain and Louis so that they look upon them almost as brothers." The shaky thread of her voice broke abruptly and Fleur felt a surge of anger against Alain when she saw how his coldness had upset her. Her fine old hands were shaking as she lifted her glass to sip a minute quantity of wine, and when she put it down again she lifted her napkin to her lips to hide their quivering.

Hoping to turn her mind into happier channels, Fleur smiled across the table and said gently, "You must have been a very lovely young bride, Maman, and I've no doubt your thoughtfulness and charm have much to do with the devotion your workers show toward your family."

Her face cleared. "How nice of you to say so, child. But no, I must not take the credit. My dear husband was a good, kind man who held the welfare of his people close to his heart. He was a true aristocrat, but he had more sympathy with his workers than many of our middle-class neighbors."

For one infinitesimal second her eyes flickered toward Célèstine and Fleur wondered uncomfortably if the Chesnaye family fell into this last category. The suspicion became stronger when she heard a slight choking sound that might have been a half-smothered laugh coming from Louis, who sat next to her, and the suspicion was clarified when an unbecoming flush ran in an angry wave across Célèstine's perfect features.

Acutely ashamed of her small breach of manners, the Comtesse quickly continued: "As I mentioned to Alain earlier today, my dear Fleur, you must not hesitate to change anything inside the château which does not please you. I remember how excited I felt when my husband gave me carte blanche to do as I wished with the interior decorations and the plans I conceived for each room as I wandered through them. For centuries, you see, the décor had been the same—renovated, of course, but always keeping to the same basic theme."

"Each room in the château has a flower motif, as you will see for yourself when I show you around. Your bedroom is the rose room, whereas mine is done in delicate shades of yellow and follows a mimosa motif. Other rooms are furnished in lavender, violet, white lily of the valley, red geranium, in fact, in the colors of every flower that grows around the château. But, strangely, when it came to the time to make changes I could not do so, and the décor has remained the same for yet another generation."

Fleur quickly assured her, "And so far as I am concerned, it will always stay that way, Maman. I think it an original and lovely idea, one I wouldn't dream of spoiling."

Attention was focused upon Célèstine when she gave a high-pitched laugh. "Original?" she mocked, still bitingly aware of the Comtesse's snub. "How can one call an idea original when it has been copied by every bride for centuries? My definition of original is something not copied; this dress I am wearing, for instance, is the only one of its kind. Unlike Fleur's," she finished maliciously, "it is not a poor imitation of the real thing!"

When this attack was followed by an appalled silence Célèstine knew she had gone too far.

Fleur felt hot color sweeping under her skin and her lashes descended to fan across her cheeks in two gold-tipped crescents thick enough to hide the humiliation in her telltale eyes. She felt grateful to Louis when he swiftly championed her.

"But, Célèstine, my love," he drawled with a mockery that infuriated her, "it never ceases to amaze me how girls like you who patronize the exclusive gown shops somehow always manage to look the same, whereas Fleur has a natural beauty that would show up to advantage if she wore sackcloth! That alone—" his tone changed to banter as he nodded in Alain's direction "—is an asset that should make any husband feel grateful."

Alain frowned, displeased at the turn the conversation had taken, while Célèstine sat silently fuming, not quick-witted enough to bandy words with the worldly Louis and resentful of the fact.

The Comtesse rose to her feet and declared firmly, "I think it is time Alain and Fleur were left to their own company. We seem to have forgotten," she looked pointedly at Célèstine, "that this has been a long and very eventful day for both of them and they must be wanting to retire early. It is, after all, their wedding night and we ought to be grateful to them for their forbearance in allowing us to share part of it with them. But now—" she moved to tap Alain sharply on the shoulder "—I insist that you take Fleur up to her room. The poor child is drooping with weariness."

Fleur's eyes were haunted when she looked immediately to see Alain's reactions to the order given with such bravery by the old Comtesse, who was even now waiting, aghast at her own daring, wondering what answer to expect from this stranger who was her son. With relief, she saw his brooding features lighten.

Probably to humor her, or perhaps as an apology for his harsh words, he had decided to obey his mother's command. Fleur heard Louis expel a relieved breath, then was startled into activity when Alain's voice cut across the room.

"Perhaps you are right, Maman, it has been a trying day and an extremely eventful one." Then his eyes roved blindly around the table as he asked, "Fleur, if you are ready, I think we should go to our rooms."

Louis jumped to his feet. "Let me help you, Alain."

"No, thank you—" the answer came close to being irritable "—Fleur will manage! *Bonne nuit*, Maman, Louis, and thank you, Célèstine, for your company this evening. As you are staying with us for a while we shall perhaps meet again at breakfast."

Her pouting bottom lip was very much in evidence when she answered shortly, "Perhaps."

As, at that moment, they were turning to leave the room, Fleur was the only one who saw Alain smile at this peevish answer, but she was too much occupied with her task of guiding him from the room to wonder about his amusement.

Outside his bedroom door they said goodnight, but he waited until she had opened her own door before stepping inside his room. He was so courteous in some respects, Fleur mused as she undressed in solitary splendor, and yet so thoughtless in others. It was impossible to read his thoughts or to gauge his reactions because of the mercurial quality of his moods.

Giving herself a mental shake, she resolved not to worry and hurried into the bathroom for a quick shower. This time she was not interrupted, and less than ten minutes later she was back in her room sliding her refreshed body between the diaphanous folds of the black nylon and lace nightdress she had chosen for her wedding night—a wicked extravagance she had bought with a catch in her throat.

It was a sultry night. She wandered across to the window and drew back the curtains protecting the night. It was dark outside, with just a weak sickle of moon and no stars to twinkle away the melancholy in her soul. She clung to the heavy drapes and dreamily absorbed the heavenly fragrances drifting up from the ocean of flowers that billowed and swayed somewhere out in the darkness. She stood, half-awake, half-dreaming, for uncountable minutes until gradually she became aware of a sound from Alain's room: the restless, monotonous sound of his feet marching backward and forward across the room. Her heart lurched at the thought that he might be ill, but she dismissed the notion when she reasoned he had only to press a bell to summon his valet if he needed assistance. As she listened, the sound formed a pattern, three steps and then the sound of a drawer closing; five steps and a light switch clicked; six steps and his door squeaked on its hinges. Suddenly the object became clear, he was pacing himself, counting each stride and memorizing where his steps led him each time. "Oh, my poor darling," she whispered brokenly, "if only you would let me help you!"

She stiffened as his footsteps halted outside the communicating door. Tears dried on her hot cheeks as she stood, hardly breathing, waiting for his next move. It was a relief to hear his light tap upon the door. "Come in!" she called out softly, her heart racing so rapidly she felt actual pain.

She had not bothered to turn on the light so his figure, clad in a dark-hued dressing gown, was hardly discernible when he stepped into the room.

"Am I intruding?" He sounded so tense she was made immediately aware of his unease. "I can't sleep," he went on, "so I was wondering—if you are not too tired—if we might talk?"

Knowing the folly of allowing him to sense pity, she strove to keep her answer light. "Of course, please come in, I can't sleep either, so we might as well keep each other company." When he walked toward her she saw his hair was tousled—run through with impatient fingers.

Under his dressing gown the top button of his pajama jacket was open revealing the strong brown column of his neck where a pulse was jerking rapidly. His nerves were as taut as coiled wire!

Calmly, she began to talk, speaking about everything and nothing, letting words ramble from her tongue at will until eventually she sensed an aura of tranquillity and fell silent, content to stand with him by the open window and let the peaceful night continue what she had begun.

"You are such a restful person, Fleur, so serene and calm. These qualities are the ones that first attracted me to you. Probably—" his voice harshened "—because of their direct opposition to my own infernal moods!"

"Hush, Alain," she soothed gently. "If only you would allow your mind to relax, your body would soon follow suit."

"If only!" he mimicked, his fists bunching. "How everyone about me must be echoing that wish! Tonight I hurt even my mother with my caustic tongue." His hand jerked out and closed around the curtain, grabbing it with such impatient strength she thought it would rip from the wall. "No one understands," he muttered through clenched teeth, "no one can comprehend the agony of trying to survive in a world of darkness. I hear voices, listen to words, and wonder all the time what hidden shades of meaning are lost by my inability to see the expression on the speaker's face. For two years I've been tormented by lies so now I distrust every word spoken to me. When I hear someone say, 'How pleased I am to see you,' I ask myself if the sentiment is accompanied by a genuine smile or with a grimace of displeasure. When I eat, I ask myself: are my table manners disgusting or can I believe those who tell me I have perfected the art of eating blind? I even distrust my mother's words, but they at least are bearable because I know she would never willingly deceive me. But what of you, Fleur?"

She was startled out of her state of frozen pity when his hands descended with force upon her lightly clad shoulders. "What am I to believe about you? I had imagined you a sweet, good person who thought only of others, but then you disconcerted me completely by admitting yourself corruptible—you were for sale and I bought you! *Mon Dieu!*" He shook her so hard she had to bite back a cry of pain. "For some reason your defection torments me far more than any other's. I need you around me, confound you, but I will not play the part of a blind beggar! Tell me the truth! Whom did I marry, the gentle daughter of a vicar, or a mercenary, scheming woman?"

She tried to shrink away, too shocked and frightened by the raw hatred that possessed him to even register that a question had been asked. The tiger she thought had been tamed, only minutes ago, had snarled back to life with a ferociousness she could neither understand nor cope with. His hands burned her shoulders with their heat and his eyes as they glittered down at her mirrored a furious hatred mere words could never hope to dispel.

Down under the wave of horror she was feeling, compassion stirred, but it was too weak an emotion to combat the fear he had aroused—a fear that turned to panic when he pulled her close against his hard body and hissed into her ear, "So you are too ashamed to answer!"

She was lifted from her feet in one swoop and carried swiftly across to the bed. She tried to gasp out a protest, but unshed tears drowned the sound in her throat. She did not attempt to struggle, but lay looking up with wide, frightened eyes at the arrogant, solitary man—blinded in mind and body—who was her lawful husband, to whom she had been joined for life that morning by her own father.

He leaned forward and she saw him smile, the white-toothed smile of a hungry predator, and a second later her hair was spread in a shower of gold across his arm and her lips were being plundered of their sweetness. He was strong in anger and bitter in mind, but as his loving progressed it drew from her shy responses that chased the iron from his soul, making his caresses become suddenly considerate, thoughtful and passionately gentle.

The pungent scent of roses detached itself from the mass and drifted through the open window, so that forever afterward the flower was a reminder of this night when from out of raging distrust and brutal force an emotion so fragile—so ethereal it could not bear description—was conceived and born within a man too blind to see what was written on his heart.

Later, as she lay still and inwardly weeping against his steadily beating heart, she wrestled with her bewildered emotions, trying to sort out joy from pain, arid emptiness from sweet fulfillment, and conflicting feelings of love and shame. Was she loved or despised? Had he taken her as a wife or a courtesan—one paid for services rendered?

He stirred, murmured her name, and tightened his arm around her. She relaxed against his warmth with a smile of contentment and closed her eyes—leaving the question still unanswered.

Chapter Seven

WHEN SHE AWOKE the next morning he was gone; only the imprint of his head against the pillow remained to convince her she had not dreamed the whole shattering experience. She tried not to dwell upon the events of the previous night, but as she fumbled with the fasteners on her dress one question kept recurring: how would he react at their next meeting?

She was sitting at her dressing table wielding her hairbrush with a shaky hand when his image appeared behind her own in the mirror, startling her so that she dropped the brush with a clatter upon the glass-topped surface.

"Did I frighten you?" he asked without a

trace of apology. He had been perfectly valeted, dressed in a light-colored suit with a matching silk shirt and an impeccably knotted tie. His dark hair was still damp from the shower.

"You could have knocked." She had striven to answer calmly, but her agitation was betrayed by a slight quaver.

Negligently he answered, "Why? I can't see you, but even if I could, does it matter—now?"

The coldness in his voice was unbearable. She jumped to her feet, her face scarlet, and made to pass him, but with keen perception he reached out and caught her by the shoulders before she could escape.

"I haven't come to apologize," he told her, his mouth grim. "What happened last night was quite unintentional, neither planned nor desired. Do you believe me?"

Somewhere deep in her heart her newly nurtured hopes died a quiet death. It seemed hardly possible that the aloof words she had heard came from the same man who only hours ago had been whispering soft French endearments against her lips and whose fierce then tender passion had introduced into her life a whole new concept of feeling.

When she did not answer, he shrugged and

released his hold. "I see you doubt me. However, it hardly matters. I shall see to it you are recompensed. I cannot afford the time to go with you to Paris, but I shall arrange with one of the fashion houses to send a selection of clothes for you to choose from. Also there are family jewels that you might like to sort through. I'll ask Maman to show them to you—she will advise whether or not they need resetting."

Each word stabbed her heart with the precision of a deliberately aimed rapier. She wondered if it was possible to die of shame, if a heart so badly wounded could bleed inwardly—and fatally—thus bringing eventual blessed oblivion. She swayed, fighting a dreadful nausea.

It was as well he could not see the havoc his words had inflicted—her slender-stemmed body was wilting, her bright head was drooping on her slender neck, and her bruised mouth was quivering with pain and disillusionment.

"Well? Why don't you answer? If there is something you would particularly like you only have to say."

She drew in a great gulping breath to steady herself, then trembled.

"I'd like to be left alone. Please will you go now?"

His eyebrows elevated with surprise at the pain in her voice, then drew back into a straight black line as puzzlement clouded his face.

His sightless eyes bored down at her, probing, questioning, seeming to strive with everything that was in him to find out the cause of her distress.

"What have I said to upset you?" he asked sharply. Then slowly, as if as an afterthought, he wondered aloud, "Can it be that I have misunderstood?"

Once more his hand clasped her shoulders and he pulled her forward with an urgency she could not combat. "Tell me again why you married me!"

Five minutes earlier she might have told him. Then, she had felt secure, wrapped around by the warm glow of what she had begun to hope might be love or, if not that, then at least some measure of regard. But now, stripped of all illusions, she would have died rather than let him guess how much she loved him.

The anger within her, self-anger at her own weakness and stupidity, helped her to play her part with conviction. Jerking herself out of his clutches, she stepped out of his reach and with a deception that inwardly horrified her she projected teasing frivolity into her answer.

"Upset? Who's upset? Really, Alain, your penchant for taking pleasures seriously disappoints me. The French, so I've been led to believe, have the reputation of being expert lovers, full of verve and completely devoid of inhibitions, but I must say you seem totally lacking in this respect. Relax, don't worry, I assure you that's what I intend to do. I refuse absolutely to allow anything to upset my enjoyment of what promises to be a delightful new future!"

Amazingly, her gallant words fooled him. As she watched, his features hardened into a mask of angry dislike that made her cower against the bed, weak with self-loathing. "I'm sorry to have been such a disappointment." His cold lips barely moved as they framed the words. "It is just as well the error will never be repeated."

"I don't understand. . . ." There was no trace of her former frivolity when she choked out the words.

"I regret my lapse—my lack of control—but what you have just said absolves me from the need to apologize. Obviously you are not the type of person to appreciate remorse; your need is for material things, and those I will willingly supply if only to wash my hands of a debt I freely admit is owing to you."

His fists bunched as he fought to contain his rage. For a second he looked as if he would say more, but then he compressed his lips to force back the words she could not have borne to hear. When the door banged behind his departing figure she sank back on the bed in a welter of despair, determined not to cry, but helpless to suppress the hard, dry sobs that racked her body.

Louis had just finished breakfast when she went downstairs half an hour later. She had bathed her hot face with water before leaving her room, and her trembling body was now under control, but every chivalrous instinct Louis possessed was aroused when he saw the haunted look that darkened her beautiful eyes. With unusual tact, he forbore to comment when he rose from his seat to offer her some breakfast.

"No, thank you, Louis." She waved away his offer with such apathy he felt an immediate fury with Alain.

He knew her well enough already to feel

sure her loyalty would never allow her to discuss her husband, not even with his cousin, but as he poured out black coffee he was resolving to seek out Alain and to take up with him the subject of her deep unhappiness.

"Thank you, Louis."

Fleur took the proffered cup and drank from it thirstily.

"Won't you please change your mind and have some croissants?" he pleaded.

She shook her head. "No, but I will have some more coffee." As he refilled her cup he noticed the way her eyes kept straying toward the door, as if dreading the appearance of Alain, and on impluse he asked, "Did Alain give you a message for me?" When she again shook her head he frowned before continuing, "I'm going down to the factory this morning. I was supposed to wait for Alain, but as he's nowhere about and he has left me no message I won't wait any longer. How would you like to come with me?"

If he had any doubts about a breach existing between his cousin and his new bride they were dispelled as soon as he saw the relief that chased across her troubled face.

Without even waiting to drink the coffee he had just poured, she jumped to her feet and stammered, "Yes, I'd love to! I'll just slip upstairs for my bag. I won't be more than a minute."

"Hold on!" Louis laughed, amused by her impatience. "What about your coffee?" But she had already gone.

At any other time she would have been entranced by the scenery they drove through on the way to the factory. The landscape was vast and refreshing, far away from cities and crowds, shops and artificial entertainment. They drove through vast flower fields—a veritable sea of flowers—mainly roses and jasmine, real jasmine whose scent filled the air with perfumed pungency. Against the background of her thoughts Louis's voice impinged, giving her odd pieces of information about the industry as he drove, mercifully content to ramble on without receiving or expecting any response.

A small part of her mind retained some of his words and afterward she was to wonder at the fact that seven hundred flowers were required for one liter of perfume—ten pounds of roses for two pounds of essence.

Absently, she exchanged waves with the pickers who straightened from their back-breaking work long enough to salute the occupants of the car as they drove past, then continued like a swarm of honey-searching bees with their task of stripping the sweetness from the blossom-laden bushes.

Louis smiled wryly when, at the mention of Alain's name, she unconsciously betrayed interest. Cursing the spasm of sudden jealousy that had speared him, and vowing not to allow himself to commit the awful folly of falling in love with his cousin's wife, he repeated the words she had missed.

"As I was saying, there are only fifteen people in the world who can distinguish between six thousand different fragrances, and at present twelve of them live in Grasse—Alain, of course, is one of them."

"And what about you, Louis?" Her smile was so full of gentle concern that it was as much as he could do to resist leaning across and kissing her.

"I'm sure you are good at your job, too, but for some reason you seem reluctant to admit it. Why, I wonder?" He grinned widely, but she was not deceived.

"Alain has always bettered me in everything we have both undertaken, so I decided it was useless to compete. It was decreed years ago that I should always be regarded as a second-best Treville," he vouchsafed a trifle bitterly.

"Alain's father and mine were twins and for the sake of a mere ten minutes in time his father inherited the château and the estate while mine had to be content with whatever was offered. I was still an infant when both my parents were killed in an air crash and my aunt, whom I have always called Maman, brought me to the château, and this is where I have lived ever since. But even during my schooldays I lived in the shadow of Alain's brilliance, just as I still do today. He is the substance and I the shadow," he ended wryly.

The forlorn note echoing through hs words distressed Fleur deeply, so much so that she leaned forward to assure him earnestly, "That's not true, Louis, and I want you to promise me you'll never think that way again." Her deep concern and the nearness of her lips, deeply pink and parted slightly with the eager innocence of a child, was his undoing and before he himself was fully aware of the intention his mouth had descended firmly upon hers in a kiss that was, to him, full of heady sweetness.

She drew away immediately, too shocked to verbally condemn him, and he had to give all his attention to the car, which had swerved momentarily out of control. When he had righted it, he sensed her disapproval and quickly apologized. "I'm sorry, Fleur, truly sorry! I did that on the spur of the moment. You were so sweet, worrying on my behalf, I simply couldn't resist you. Please, will you forgive me?"

For the first time in his life he was genuinely worried about being out of favor with a member of the opposite sex. Fleur, to him, had begun to represent all the things he had once looked for in a woman, looked for and then reluctantly abandoned after deciding he was searching for a myth, a member of a nonexistent species.

The agony of it was that, now he had found her, she belonged to the one man in the world whose property he dared not touch—his cousin. A cousin, moreover, who was incapable of feelings other than anger and cynical scorn and who, judging from Fleur's unhappy face, treated his wife with the same lack of concern as he did the rest of the family.

Louis's alien look of worry convinced Fleur he was feeling abjectly sorry for his lapse, which she generously put down to youthful indiscretion, so she forgave him instantly. "All right, I forgive you, but don't let it happen again!" she admonished, hating the misery she saw on his downcast face. It was only when she saw his lips quirk with amusement and the twinkle reappear in his eyes that she realized how prim she must have sounded—like a schoolmarm reproaching a recalcitrant child—and her mouth trembled into an answering smile.

In a second, the ice was broken and they both began to chuckle. Louis's mirth overcame him to such an extent that he had to pull in at the side of the road and for several uproarious minutes they were helpless with laughter.

He was the first to regain control. He wiped his streaming eyes and struggled for composure in order to tell her, "Thank you, *ma belle* Fleur, I enjoyed that; a day without laughter is a day wasted!"

Fleur, her eyes shining and with all unhappy thoughts scattered to the four winds, smiled back serenely and agreed. "I needed it, too, Louis. It has helped me enormously."

"Then I am glad to have been of service," he answered, sobering quickly at the memory of her previous unhappiness. "I must keep it in mind to kiss you more often, especially when you are depressed."

She laughed, secure in the conviction that he was still fooling, and settled back in her seat, prepared to enjoy the remainder of the journey.

They were still in a happy, laughing mood when they reached Grasse. He drove along the Boulevard du Jeu de Ballon, a delightful road shaded from the heat of the sun by rows of plane trees, then let the car coast gently down a slope leading to a terrace-shaped promendade where he parked in a spot that gave a splendid view of the surroundings of Cannes and the flower fields. Flinging out an arm to encompass everything in sight, he asked her with the triumph of a little boy who has saved the best treat to the last, "Well, what do you think of the view?"

"It's awe-inspiring, magnificent . . . oh, I can't find sufficient adjectives," she admitted, much to his pleasure.

"Listen, Fleur, I don't have to go to the factory just yet. Let me show you around the old parts of the city, I'm sure you'll love it. Afterward, we'll have lunch at a hotel I know where they make the best *bouillabaise* in the region. What do you say, are you agreeable?"

She needed very little persuasion. The sun was hot, the sky vividly blue, and Louis was a very pleasant companion. Besides that, there was always the chance that she might run into Alain at the factory.

Bright-eyed, she nodded, and he showed his delight by raising her hand to his lips and kissing the tips of her fingers. For a moment she felt a slight unease, for behind his innocent expression she had glimpsed a worldliness that would not have shamed a man twice his age, but in a trice his boyish look returned and with it a renewal of the trust she placed in him.

Happily, she allowed him to help her out of the car and then hand in hand they wandered along to the end of the promenade where they descended large steps that led into the main street of the old city.

He proved himself to be an excellent guide. Speaking knowledgeably on every subject, he pointed out the eighteenth-century houses with their irregular-shaped colonnades, the memorial in the center of old Grasse that he told her had been sculpted by Bourgeois, explored with her an incredibly old, early Gothic cathedral, then took her along a maze of quaint streets that had houses built on slopes with stone steps leading up to the front doors, each step containing boxes of flowering plants that cascaded down to the street in colorful profusion.

Outside some of the houses old ladies in long black dresses covered with spotlessly white pinafores and with starched caps of white muslin protecting their heads from the sun sat chatting to their neighbors, or watching over young children playing happily in the dusty street. Fleur was fascinated by everything she saw and would have lingered for hours among the legion of tiny, cluttered shops displaying everything from pots and pans to antique jewelry and paintings.

She was astonished when Louis reminded her, "We'll have to make our way back if we are to have lunch before going on to the factory, but I'll bring you back here another day when we have more time and let you browse to your heart's content."

"Gracious!" she gasped, "are you sure we have time for lunch? Shouldn't we go straight to the factory in case you're needed there?" But he was adamantly determined not to forgo the pleasure of introducing her to his favorite meal, so she did not argue and they made their way back along the promenade to where the restaurant was situated.

The *bouillabaisse*—a delicious fish

soup—was excellent and so filling that she could not attempt to eat a second course. To please Louis, she sipped a small amount of the liqueur he had ordered especially to tempt her appetite, but its licorice taste did not appeal to her and she left most of it in her glass. Her enjoyment began to wane when, after an hour and a half, he was still making no move to depart. Gently, she hinted that she wanted to leave, but half of the carafe of wine he had ordered still waited to be drunk and with a sinking feeling of dread she began to realize he had no intention of leaving until it was finished.

It was late afternoon when finally she managed to coax him out of the restaurant. She bit her lip when he staggered slightly on his way to the car, but she said nothing, wary of the belligerent, argumentative mood that had overtaken him as gradually as the wine had emptied from the bottle. She was sick with worry when, after a hair-raising drive, they finally pulled up with a squeal of brakes outside of a large brick building that had Maison Treville scrawled across its front in gold letters.

In her eagerness to get out of the car, Fleur did not notice another car slide silently to a halt behind them. She spun around on her heel when Célèstine's voice reached her.

"So here you both are! I've searched over all of Grasse to find you!" She ran the tip of her tongue over her lips and smiled with such venom Fleur was repelled. "Alain," she said, raking Fleur's face with obvious enjoyment, "is furious with you!"

They left a suddenly sober Louis to make his own way into the factory, and Fleur followed Célèstine up a flight of stone steps that led, Célèstine informed her, to the laboratories where Alain and she had been working all morning.

Célèstine left her in no doubt of her satisfaction with this arrangement.

"I drove Alain down from the château after we were told you and Louis had left earlier. Of course, we expected to find you here when we arrived. Alain had decided to continue his work on his unfinished project, but as he naturally has to have someone to measure and weigh the ingredients for him, and as you were not available, I offered my services—a better arrangement, really, because he trained me years ago to help him with his work, and you, my dear, would have been more of a hindrance than a help, if you don't mind me saying so."

Fleur made no reply, so she carried on complacently.

"There is another reason why I want to help him finish this particular job. The creation he is working on is a masterpiece; it was almost finished when the accident happened, and only small adjustments were needed before Alain would admit himself satisfied. Then—" she drew in a deep breath of satisfaction "—the creation was to be mine, my own personal perfume devised exclusively for me by Maison Treville!"

By this time they had reached the top of the stairs, but before opening the door leading into the laboratory Célèstine halted, determined that Fleur should fully understand her importance in Alain's life.

"You will find Alain a little distrait, *ma chérie*. About lunchtime he began to betray signs of annoyance at your prolonged absence—and Louis's," she added delicately. "But you must try not to mind his jealousy, because once before he thought he had cause to suspect someone he loved of being unfaithful to him and he has never completely trusted anyone since."

"Someone he loved?" Fleur repeated gravely. "Would that someone be you, Célèstine?"

"You know!" She sounded surprised. "Did Louis tell you?" When Fleur nodded her expression changed. Fleur was completely taken in by the sudden look of hurt vulnerability that swept over her face. Her lovely mouth was trembling with hurt when she whispered, "It hurts even to think of it. Alain and I were to have been married only a month later. The day before his accident he was told by someone whose name I have yet to discover that I had a . . . lover."

Her voice broke on the word, but she straightened as if determining to finish the tale, and carried on bravely. "It was a lie, of course, from the moment we became engaged I never gave a second thought to any other man, but the damage had been done. Alain refused to believe me and he broke off our engagement." Fleur's eyes widened with bewilderment and Célèstine hurried on as if sensing that she was about to be interrupted. "Oh, it was made to look as if I did the jilting, to spare my feelings, he said at the time, but it was he nevertheless who was responsible for ending our engagement. He refused to discuss the matter with anyone—not even his mother—and nothing I said made the slightest difference. His mind was made up. So now you understand—" her eyes raked Fleur's face, seeking to read her very mind "—why you must be very careful what you do and say to Alain. He is very sensitive of his position and very, very jealous of his possessions."

Fleur was shocked, appalled to think even Alain capable of such intolerance and unable to understand how he could have taken the word of a stranger against that of the girl who was to have become his wife. Célèstine seemed so sincere it was impossible to disbelieve her. How could Alain, who must have loved her deeply, have refused to listen when she had attempted to explain? Why should he have become so embittered, so suspicious of everyone's motives?

From out of the past her father's words echoed in her mind: "The man has turned into an insensible automaton. I feel he has been hurt so often—and perhaps not merely physically—that he has determined never to allow himself to feel ever again!"

Her hand went to her mouth to stifle a gasp of pain, pain for Alain whose mental torment at his believed betrayal must have scarred him deeper than the incisions inflicted upon him physically.

She had suspected him of having other reasons besides the one he had mentioned for marrying her, and her suspicions had been correct. He had wanted to hit back at Célèstine for her supposed deception, to show her how little he cared about her.

He had deliberately sought a wife—any wife—so that he could confront Célèstine with a *fait accompli*, someone who would be a buttress against the attraction she must still hold for him, someone dependable who would fill the gap she had left in his life. She gasped as realization hit her. She had let him down! This morning he had needed her to help him with his work and he had had to fall back on Célèstine's offer of help!

"Where is Alain? I must go to him." She sounded so agitated that Célèstine automatically moved out of the way to allow her to pass through the door. "Please," Fleur implored when she made to follow, "I'd like to speak to him alone."

Célèstine's eyes narrowed, but the flash of stubbornness revealed by Fleur's out-thrust chin warned her not to argue, so she shrugged and began descending the stairs. "Very well, I'll be with Louis when Alain asks for me," she warned defiantly, daring Fleur to try to dispel

138

the growing accord between herself and Alain. But Fleur had already disappeared into the laboratory in search of him.

She found him talking to an earnest young man in a white jacket who was very carefully weighing a small amount of fluid from out of a brown glass bottle. Tiers of such bottles, each marked with a chemical formula, were ranged around the workbench within easy reach, and Fleur remembered hearing Louis describe it as a "keyboard," a library of odors from which the perfumier selected, weighed and measured the ingredients he planned to use in his experiments.

Test tubes, petri dishes and beakers were scattered around the workbench, which was covered with an opal glass top and faced a wall covered from floor to ceiling with white tiles. It was her first visit to a laboratory, and as she gazed around she felt rather disappointed by the thought of glamorous, enchanting perfumes being conceived in such clinical surroundings.

When the young man spoke to Alain and nodded in her direction she knew he was telling him of her presence.

Alain stiffened, answered him without turning, and the young man gave her an apologetic look, took off his working jacket and walked out through another door, leaving them alone together.

With all the timid earnestness of a child who knows she has done wrong and is anxious to be forgiven, she stammered an apology.

"I'm sorry I'm so late. Perhaps I should have told you I was leaving with Louis this morning—then you could have explained that you needed my help—but I simply didn't think."

He swung around, his proud head arrogantly tilted, his flaring nostrils denoting icy displeasure, and stabbed out accusingly, "You didn't think—or you thought too much? I am well aware of my cousin's attraction for the opposite sex. He is, as you have no doubt discovered, the epitome of the ideal you cherish of dashing, uninhibited young Frenchmen. Unfortunately for you, there is one commodity he lacks—money! Louis's allowance stretches no farther than his own extravagant commitments, so if you are thinking of tapping his resources I must advise you now that you'll be wasting your time!"

His words were a slap in the face, and Fleur, her eyes enormous with hurt, recoiled from them as if from a physical blow. Choking back the denial she knew would fall upon deaf ears, she stood rooted with shock watching his lips twist with a bitterness she hated. Dully, she recognized the futility of putting into words the need she had felt to reassure him of her loyalty, to make him believe how much she regretted the impulse that had driven her to seek Louis's company rather than his own. Desperation urged her almost to the brink of an explanation, but once more his words cut through her hopes.

Turning impatiently back to his workbench, he groped for an object just out of reach and when his hand did not immediately alight upon it he bit out an expletive and threw savagely across his shoulder, "I need Célèstine! Get her for me immediately, if you please, then ask someone to drive you back to the château. Not Louis," he commanded sharply. "I need him here! We have much ground to make up and I do not want you to discourage him from his work!"

Fleur fought to instill dignity into her voice, but could not entirely suppress an unsteady quaver. "Very well, I'll do as you ask. But you have no need to warn me against becoming a nuisance. I never intended keeping Louis from his work, nor do I intend keeping you from yours. Goodbye, Alain."

She blinked away scalding tears and dared

the tremor in her voice to worsen. "I'll see to it that Célèstine knows she is needed before I leave."

FOR DAYS AFTERWARD she avoided him whenever possible, going down to breakfast only when she was sure the car taking himself, Louis and Célèstine to the factory had driven away. In the mornings she made her way down to the plantations where the masses of flowers and the friendly pickers, who greeted her vociferously, were a delight. As Alain, Louis and Célèstine did not return to the château until just before dinner, she and the Comtesse had lunch together each day, after which they sat in the garden for an hour and talked before the old lady retired to her room for her afternoon nap. They were becoming very close; the Comtesse's growing affection, which she was at pains to make obvious, was a balm to Fleur's hurt feelings and she returned the old lady's regard with an eagerness that was partly due to the Comtesse's charm and understanding and partly to the intense loneliness that caught her by the throat whenever she remembered her own parents and the abundance of love with which they had surrounded her.

It was during one of their lunchtime chats that the Comtesse revealed her awareness that all was not well between her son and his bride. They were sitting together in the garden, chatting desultorily, with a musically tinkling fountain playing in the background, when the Comtesse leaned forward to peer bright-eyed into Fleur's face.

"You are not happy, child," she stated flatly, her mouth stern. "I had hoped your sunny disposition would rub off on Alain, but instead the reverse is happening and his misery is penetrating your soul. Don't deny it, *ma chérie*," she rapped out when Fleur tried to protest. "You try very hard to appear at ease, but in repose your sweet face is troubled, far more so than a bride of two weeks has any right to be. My son is a difficult husband, *n'est-ce pas?*" Fleur became suddenly white and the Comtesse hastened to apologize. "Forgive me for hurting you, *ma petite*. My probing is unforgivable!"

"It's quite all right, Maman." Fleur managed to smile. "I know how you worry about Alain and how much you desire his happiness. It is unfortunate, but I'm afraid he will never find the happiness you wish for him, at least not with me."

"If not with you, then with no one!" the Comtesse replied with such conviction Fleur was momentarily heartened. Then the old lady sighed.

"I wish I could reprimand Alain on your account; his neglect of you is unpardonable. But he is not the son I once knew—kind, lovable, one I would never hesitate to approach. Iron has entered his soul and, though I'm loath to admit it, I feel the son I knew and loved is lost to me forever."

"No! Never allow yourself to think that, Maman!"

Fleur was surprised at the strength of her own conviction. "He could be himself again if only he could see. If we could convince him that only one more operation would be necessary!"

The Comtesse caught a little of Fleur's enthusiasm and her face brightened. "Then we must try, *ma chérie*. We must both try! There must be some way of convincing him, and between us we shall find it." Her slender, finely veined hand reached out to clasp Fleur's, communicating renewed optimism, and Fleur found her own hopes miraculously revived by the effort she had made to dispel the Comtesse's despondency.

With rising excitement, she began to marshal her thoughts. Alain was not omnipotent; somewhere in his armor there had to be a chink and it was up to her to find it, whatever the cost to herself. He could destroy her, because in loving him she had given him that power, but if in destroying her he should find happiness for himself then the sacrifice would be justified. The Comtesse's voice reached through her glow of enthusiasm.

"How wonderful it would be to have my son restored to me. Once, Alain was a constant reminder of my dear husband. They were so alike in every respect it was as if part of him had never left me. That is why I felt doubly deprived by the accident that robbed Alain not only of his sight, but also of his generous, loving nature. My husband," she mused, lost in the past, "was a man of volatile feelings—his loving could take the form of tender consideration or violent rage. In a matter of seconds, if something happened to make him think it justified, he could sweep into a storm of jealousy devastating in its intensity." She laughed softly, her eyes tender with memories. "Then afterward, he would be contrite, ashamed of his lack of control, but always his favorite excuse would be: 'Consider it not as a lapse but as a compliment to yourself, because if I did not love so acutely I would not feel so acutely.'

"What woman," the Comtesse appealed, "could resist the logic of such a statement? He was so vibrant, so vitally alive, he found it impossible to repress his natural inclinations—not like Alain," she sighed sadly, "whose balance of feeling weighs down so heavily on the side of rage and icy displeasure that one wonders if the gentler emotions are lacking entirely."

For a moment while they both struggled with the depression her words had engendered there was deep silence. Then, suddenly, the Comtesse drew a sharp breath. Fleur looked up quickly, alarmed by the sound, and saw that the Comtesse was smiling, a pert smile whose mischievous glint was echoed in her eyes.

"I have it!" She snapped her fingers with the vivacity of a young girl; then, at the sight of Fleur's obvious puzzlement, she laughed excitedly and startled her still further by commanding: "You must make Alain jealous!"

"Jealous?" she stammered, completely bewildered. "But why . . . how?"

"Because," the Comtesse answered firmly,

"that way you will prove to yourself—and to him—that he is not the unfeeling automaton he tries to be! Jealousy," she insisted triumphantly, "is the twin of love. If you arouse one you must surely arouse the other!"

Fleur's heart sank. The Comtesse made it sound so easy, whereas the situation between herself and Alain was not half so uncomplicated as the old lady thought. To her, it was merely a case of jolting Alain out of the despair she thought was an aftermath of his accident.

She had no idea that not even attraction, much less love, had been part of their strange alliance, and Fleur knew she could not break the promise to Alain never to allow his mother to discover the real reasons behind their marriage.

Gently, she tried to dissuade her. "I'm afraid your plan won't work, Maman. Alain would never be jealous on my account. For one thing, I see very little of him now, and even if I did he has no cause to feel jealous when he knows I spend most of my time with you and the rest in the plantations."

"Hmm," the Comtesse pondered. "We must consider taking Louis into our confidence. I know a situation such as this will appeal to his sense of humor and he is always ready to indulge in a prank. Yes, we must certainly ask for Louis's advice."

Fleur felt the situation was getting out of hand and that now was the time to put her foot down, but before she could assemble her arguments the Comtesse took the initiative. "We must also entertain!" She rose from her seat and began pacing backward and forward, her enthusiasm in full flood.

"Our neighbors and friends are eager to welcome Alain home and they are especially eager to meet you, my dear. I have put them off with the excuse that you are both still at the honeymoon stage, but news that Alain is working each day at the distillery must by now have spread all over Grasse, so when I put it to him he will not be able to refuse to go along with my plan for a dinner party." She stopped dead, her tiny figure alive with suppressed excitement, and asked Fleur abruptly, "Well, do you dare?"

Fleur, to her own dismay, was incapable of disheartening her. Struggling to submerge the trepidation she felt, she stared mutely back at her.

Then, when the Comtesse tapped her foot impatiently, she whispered, "Very well, if you think it will do any good . . . I'll try."

The Comtesse's rigid frame relaxed. "Good!" she said simply. "Alain cannot fail to find you lovable, *chérie,* and when we have finished our campaign to rout his morbid self-pity he will be so anxious to regain his sight that he will allow nothing to stand in his way."

"Oh, I do hope you are right, Maman. I do hope so!" Fleur cried.

The Comtesse leaned forward to take her chin between her hands, and when she saw tears glistening in the velvet blueness of her eyes she derided softly, "No tears, *ma petite!* I shall excuse them only if they are tears of joy. Come, dry your eyes. I have something to show you." She urged her to her feet and shooed her in the direction of the house. "Alain left instructions this morning that you were to be shown the family jewels so that you might choose from them the pieces you prefer. I had forgotten, but now that I have remembered I'm sure you'll see his request as I do—as a good omen for the future, *n'est-ce pas?*"

No, not so! Fleur wanted to scream as she followed her down the passageway to the library.

Quite unknowingly the Comtesse had plunged a dagger into her heart; how distressed she would be if she knew she had been delegated by her son to pay his wife the first installment of the debt he considered was owing to her.

Chapter Eight

THERE WERE PEARLS, milk white and perfectly matched, made up into a necklace of three strands long enough to have reached her waist. A pearl and diamond set comprising tiara, necklace, earrings and bracelet, so magnificent they could be worn only at functions of royal proportions, nestled against a background of black velvet. And an abundance of rubies, sapphires and emeralds mounted in settings of fine gold were fashioned into a fabulous assortment of rings, bracelets and brooches. The Comtesse took them all from a concealed safe in the library, and as she opened the caskets one by one to lay them on a table for inspection Fleur drew back from their magnificence with a dislike that amounted to near repugnance. She hated each and every one of the beautiful things. In different circumstances she might have delighted in the richness of color, in the purity of design, but as it was each pearl represented a tear, each diamond echoed the cold hardness of Alain's eyes.

Lovingly, the Comtesse displayed the Treville family's treasures, now and then holding up to the light some particularly fine piece so that the sunshine flooding the room delved into the heart of the stones, making them burst forth with scintillating, colorful brilliance.

"Well?" The Comtesse cocked her head on one side as she queried, "Which pieces do you most admire, *chérie?*"

"They are all gorgeous, Maman," she stammered, "but they are much too lavish for me to wear. I should be terrified of losing them."

"Nonsense!" the Comtesse answered fondly. "As the Comtesse de Treville you will soon become accustomed to wearing fine stones. Our neighbors entertain extensively and you will be expected to return their hospitality. Such occasions are welcomed by the womenfolk because they give them an excuse to dress up as well as being a help in prizing husbands away from their all-absorbing work. So you see there will be plenty of opportunity for you to wear your jewels. Come, let us decide together which pieces will best flatter your delicate coloring."

But not even to please the Comtesse could she evince sufficient enthusiasm, and the old lady was quick to sense her lack of interest. After debating at length upon the merits of each stone and receiving very lukewarm response, she began with a perplexed shrug to replace the jewels in their caskets, snapping back the catches with a sharpness that emphasized her disappointment.

Conscious of her hurt feelings, Fleur tried to make amends. Lying in the bottom of one of the jewel cases, looking as forlorn and out of place among its grand companions as she felt herself, was a small blue enameled charm on a fine gold chain.

She reached out with pretended eagerness to lift the small object from the depths of the jewel case.

"I . . . I like this very much."

She sounded so contrite that the Comtesse had to respond with a smile as she took the bauble from her.

"This? But it is almost worthless, child!

Louis bought it for me years ago, when he was a mere boy—a birthday present, I think—and for all these years it has lain here overlooked." She dangled the chain from her finger so that the charm flashed blue in the sunlight.

"Then, of course, you must keep it," Fleur told her awkwardly, wishing she had never glimpsed its cool beauty.

"Certainly not," the Comtesse smiled fondly, "I'm pleased you have found something to your taste, my dear. See!" She pointed out an inscription traced inside the charm, *"Unis mais toujours séparés."* When her eyebrows were raised inquiringly, the Comtesse translated: "Together but always apart." Fleur's heart jerked painfully. What mischievous fate had ordained that she should pick out the one thing that expressed so aptly the situation existing between Alain and herself?

The low neckline of the cream-colored silk dress she wore that evening cried out for a trinket to relieve its severity and the little blue charm fulfilled the purpose admirably. It nestled against the tender smoothness of her skin, making itself an immediate part of her, rising and falling gently with each breath she drew, its poignant message hidden from sight but emblazoned in letters of fire across her heart. "Together, but always apart!" She and Alain had become as one; his heart had beaten against hers with a wildness that even now brought a tremor to her vulnerable mouth and an urgent wave of yearning through her suddenly weak body. For the space of a few short hours she had been completely his and she had had his undivided attention.

If, for the rest of her lifetime, she had only that one night to remember she would have no regrets, because however far apart they were to become in the future she would have those moments of complete unity to sustain her. She closed her eyes, shutting out the sight of her own agony reflected in the mirror, and sat for long moments battling with tears that sprang from a seemingly never ending source.

Alain's entrance was noiseless. His presence hit her with the force of a blow when his voice resounded across her shoulder.

"I have been speaking with my mother. She tells me none of the jewels are to your liking?"

She spun around, her hand going immediately to the little blue charm, clinging to it as if to a talisman that would protect her from his anger. Her throat ached as she forced out the answer.

"On the contrary, they are all much too beautiful and too costly for me ever to wear with comfort. You must remember that I am a country girl, unused to such opulence, and you must give me time to adjust."

Expecting a sarcastic rejoinder, she held her breath, but his voice when he spoke was unfamiliar—run through with tenderness.

"Poor, meek little girl, don't you like living from the top of the bottle?" Wary of his unaccustomed gentleness, her blue eyes distended with alarm.

When he moved to touch her she stepped out of reach so hastily she overturned a stool, projecting it against the dressing table with a crash that set bottles and jars jangling. Like a sword into a scabbard, his hand was quickly sheathed.

Blind remorse filled her. She stepped forward to touch him—to communicate without words—but even as she moved his darkly handsome face clouded and his mouth tightened into a line of arrogant scorn.

"You have no need to run from me!" he accused, his dark eyes glittering. "I came, at my mother's request, because she had formed the opinion that I am neglecting you. She, naturally, is not aware that you prefer my neglect to my attention and I would not wish her to know." Ignoring her attempt to stammer an objection, he went on, "She has willed me into agreeing to yet another plan for which I have promised support. We are to give a dinner party—rather a formal one, I'm afraid—so that our friends and neighbors might be introduced to the new Comtesse de Treville. My mother will help you arrange it, she is an expert hostess and you will learn much from her. I shall be too busy during the next couple of weeks to be of much help, but I'm certain you and Maman together will be able to cope. It should, at least, alleviate some of the pressure she is bringing to bear upon me regarding my neglect of you, and it will also be a good opportunity for you to begin adjusting to your new position. Everyone, therefore—" his words became heavily charged with sarcasm "—should then be completely happy."

Fleur thought, as she scanned his grim face, that she had never seen anyone looking less happy.

It seemed that not even Célèstine's constant companionship, nor the return of their former friendliness, was enough to drive the demons from his soul.

"We will go downstairs together," he gritted, holding out his arm with such surety in her direction that she thought he must have built-in radar where she was concerned. She took it without a murmur, laying her fingertips so lightly against his white-jacketed arm that it seemed impossible he should be aware they were there.

But the muscles under his sleeve responded immediately to her touch, knotting as if to control any stray impulse that might lead to a softening that could be construed as intimacy.

During dinner Fleur was reminded of the scheme the Comtesse had evolved that afternoon.

It was obvious that she had lost no time in acquainting Louis with the facts, because as soon as they were seated at the table he began to flirt outrageously, flinging himself into the act with an enjoyment that was not all manufactured.

Holding her eyes with his, he leaned across and whispered penetratingly, "How flattered I am that you have chosen to wear my small contribution to the Treville treasury, *ma petite*. Do you like it for itself alone, or did the fact that I bought it have a bearing on your choice?"

She was taken completely by surprise and before she could form a reply the Comtesse spoke to her.

Without so much as an ashamed blink, she informed everyone, "Fleur fell in love with the charm as soon as she saw it, Louis. Every other stone was discarded in favor of the little blue charm you bought me so many years ago. You do not mind that I have given it to Fleur?"

"Mind? I am delighted, Maman! Its wearer has brought it to life, enchanted it with her beauty so that it rises and falls with every beat of her heart. How I envy it its resting place."

His wicked enjoyment of the situation sent the blood rushing to Fleur's cheeks. She tried not to look at Alain, but when she finally succumbed to the urge she wished she had not, because although he seemed to be listening calmly, even disinterestedly, she noticed that the hand holding his fork was showing white at the knuckles and the other was clasping and unclasping in the manner she had long since learned was an indication of savagely held restraint.

Célèstine, ever vigilant, seized upon the situation to twist it to her advantage. With her eyes trained upon Fleur's confused face, she mocked, "Poor Fleur, you must not let Louis embarrass you so. He is an expert philanderer, never to be taken seriously, and especially not by a girl as unsophisticated as yourself. Although I must admit, Louis—" her brilliant glance speared him "—your teasing does have an uplifting effect. Fleur's flushed cheeks and bright eyes are very becoming, don't you think?"

Unwittingly, Célèstine had helped along their cause and the Comtesse was delighted. "Indeed they are," she hastened to agree, "and you do seem to have the gift of cheering her up, Louis. Fleur always seems so happy in your company."

"And I in hers," he returned smoothly, one wicked eyelid closing in a wink as he met her glance across the table. "It has always been my pleasure to indulge beautiful women, and my new cousin's loveliness is unique." With sudden cruelty he taunted Alain, "How maddening it must be, dear cousin, to have a wife whose beauty earns you the envy of every man and yet to be unable to enjoy your ownership to the full. If I were in your shoes—" his voice softened meaningfully "—I would not rest until I could look upon what is mine."

"Louis!" His name, uttered in reproof, was the Comtesse's warning that he had gone too far, but he shrugged, unrepentant, and ignored her unspoken warning. "Well, Alain, do you feel as I do, or are you immune to the frustrations that bedevil the common man?"

Alain folded his napkin with great deliberation, making them keenly aware that the limit of his control had almost been reached. Fleur's shocked eyes were upon his face when his lips moved to eject words born of an anger so great he could barely keep his voice steady. "If you were me, Louis? But that wish is not newly conceived, is it? It is one that has plagued you for a lifetime! If you were me, you would be in control of the business and would find limitless funds to squander! Again, if you were me, you would sell this château, regardless of sentiment, and travel the world in search of pleasure! How fortunate for us all that you are not me," he bit out with ill-contained fury, "as you will never be allowed to get your hands on the business, on the château or—" his eyes flashed cold flame "—on my wife."

Fleur jumped to her feet, appalled and sickened by the stark bitterness revealed between the two men.

"No, Alain, you must not say such things! You've misunderstood—Louis is only trying to help—"

"*Himself!*" He turned on her savagely,

daring her to contradict further. She would have taken up the challenge—Louis might be weak, but he was not the villain Alain had portrayed and it would have been less than justice not to have defended him—but the Comtesse intervened with a command that demanded all the respect due to her age and to the position she had occupied for the greater part of her life.

"Alain! Louis!" Her thin old voice was as inflexible as steel. "You will put an end to this disgraceful scene immediately!"

But with unheeding fury the cousins rose to their feet, their stance antagonistic. Lithe, tensed to spring, they could have been the spirits of bygone Trevilles, each reaching instinctively to his side for the sword that would revenge their outraged cavalier instincts. The old Comtesse's frame was rigid as silently she willed them to obey her command. Célèstine's eyes glistened with enjoyment as she reveled in excitement seldom experienced within the ultracivilized circle in which she moved.

Then into the overstretched silence broke a sob Fleur failed to suppress and at the sound Louis swung in her direction, looking contrite and faintly ashamed. When her lips moved, silently forming the words "Please, Louis!" he

forced back his anger, then managed a short
laugh that did not quite project amusement.
Lightly, his flippancy belied by a wry expression Alain could neither see nor sense, he
conceded defeat.

"Forgive me, Alain, I spoke out of turn, and
for that I must apologize."

Alain did not relax; on the contrary, he
seemed savagely disappointed at being
thwarted of his prey. If he had held a sword it
would have been thrown to the ground as a
measure of his disgust, but as an alternative he
chose merely to acknowledge Louis's apology
with one terse nod of his proud head before
reaching out his hand toward the ever ready
Célèstine so that she might accompany him
from the room.

When the door closed behind them, Louis
sank down upon his chair with an exaggerated
attitude of exhaustion.

"Whew!" He expelled a relieved breath. "I
thought for one awful moment that we were
about to exchange blows! Please, Maman," he
begged the distrait Comtesse, "if you have any
more ideas for arousing Alain's emotions
please leave me out of them. I'd much prefer to
tease a slumbering tiger than go through that
again!"

But the Comtesse was not amused by his

banter. Lowering her shaking frame into a chair, she faced him across the table and accused sternly, "You were very cruel to Alain, Louis—deliberately and callously cruel—and that I find hard to forgive. Why did you taunt him so?"

Her voice trembled as she fought back the tears. "Why, Louis?"

Dull color ran under his skin as he shifted uneasily under her reproachful gaze. He tried to answer, ruffled his hair with an impatient hand, then began, shamefaced, on his defense. "I reasoned that the only way his armor could be pierced was by taunting him with his affliction," he confessed. When Fleur caught a pained breath, he swung toward her and challenged, "Well, it worked, did it not? Anything else I might have said would merely have scratched the surface of his damnable aloofness, not pierced it!" He swung back to his aunt, his anger rising at the condemnation he saw in both their faces. "That, or so I understood, was the object of the exercise. Do I now stand condemned because of my success?"

His belligerence, fierce though it was, did not quite cover up his bewilderment and Fleur responded quickly to the hurt he was trying so hard to hide.

Gently, she placed her hand on his sleeve to convey her sympathy before attempting to explain, "It was not so much your words as your actions that upset Maman. It was horrible—" a shudder ran through her body at the recollection "—to see you prepared to fight your cousin—your *blind* cousin, Louis!"

He blanched before answering, "I understand." It was a flat statement, spoken without a trace of shame, but they were left feeling he had more to say, so they remained silent. After a few minutes of introspection he threw out his arms in a gesture of helplessness and appealed, "It's his damned arrogance. It makes me forget that he is blind! Sometimes, when I see him striding down the stairs or walking unhesitantly to his chair I wonder if he really is blind or if he is perhaps having a tremendous joke at our expense!" When both of them made to interrupt, he shrugged off their protests.

"Oh, yes, I know, I know, it simply is not possible! He is blind, and I'm ashamed of the way I provoked him just now, but explain to me if you can how he does it. Can it be that he possesses some extra sense that we lesser mortals lack?"

Fleur answered his defiant question by saying simply, "He counts."

"Counts?" Louis was startled.

She nodded. "Yes, he counts. Everywhere he walks with such assurance has already been paced out in secret so that he knows exactly how many steps will be needed to reach his goal." Louis was speechless. "I've heard him," Fleur continued unknowingly betraying her own agony. "Night after night when he thinks everyone is asleep he paces the passageways, his bedroom, the stair—always counting, retracing his steps time after time until he is satisfied that he can find his way without stumbling."

"*Mon Dieu!*" Louis croaked, his eyes fastened upon her calm face. "What endurance . . . and what courage!"

The Comtesse intervened, her eyes bright with unshed tears. "None of us has ever doubted the existence of that. Whatever else Alain might lack he has proved he has courage in abundance." There was a short moment when Fleur thought the Comtesse's iron control would break, but after a visible struggle she lifted her head to display a bright smile. "Well, *mes enfants*," she directed them both, "we must not allow tonight's scene to weaken our determination to overcome Alain's resistance. By keeping in mind what you, Louis, have managed to prove—that the battlements can be breached—we must remain as resolute as ever to penetrate Alain's armored shell. Are we all agreed? You, Fleur? And you, Louis?"

Louis's impish look returned as his volatile nature responded to the challenge. "Very well, *mon Colonel*," he mocked, sketching a gay salute.

But when the Comtesse's imperious, demanding look was trained upon Fleur she blushed wild carnation, and forced herself to stammer painfully, "I . . . I'm willing to try . . . if you are quite sure it will help Alain."

Chapter Nine

FLEUR WAS ON HER WAY to the flower planta-
tion. For more than three weeks she had been
kept busy helping the Comtesse with the many
arrangements necessary for the success of the
dinner party to be held that evening, and now,
the first chance she had had, she was hurrying
to renew her acquaintance with the many
friends she had made among the pickers. The
Provençal peasant folk had taken to her
warmly, delighted with the genuine interest she
had shown toward themselves and their
families, and Fleur, in return, was rewarded by
a feeling of homecoming when at every visit
she inquired after each one's ailments, real or

imaginary, just as she had done during the parish visits she had undertaken on behalf of her father.

They were hard workers, these people of Provence. They toiled from dawn to dusk during the successive harvest seasons that went on almost all the year round, reaping the blossoms from the great terraced plantations and from the great gardens lower down, filling sacks that were then loaded into wagons ready to be hauled to the distilleries so that the soul of the gorgeous harvest could be extracted and sent, in the form of oils and essences, to the four corners of the world.

It was early afternoon and very hot. As she hurried along the path Fleur smiled to herself, remembering how only half an hour earlier the Comtesse had insisted upon sending her to her room to rest after remarking that she was looking peaky and disturbingly pale. She had had quite a job convincing her that she felt perfectly well and was not sickening for anything, but eventually she had given in to the Comtesse's urging and had been glad to go to her room to escape her fussing.

But it was such a beautiful day—the sky a hot sheet of blue with the surrounding countryside displayed like a bridesmaid's bouquet against its uncrumpled backcloth, the thrusting cypress trees throwing a circle of relieving greenery around the colorful mass—that she had not been able to resist the urge to be out of doors.

Her springing steps faltered as disturbing thoughts intruded, acting as a depressant upon her usually sunny nature. She had been married for almost four weeks now and for three of those weeks she had seen Alain only infrequently, a glimpse of his straight back as she watched him each morning from her bedroom window being driven to the factory and again in the evening, very late, because since the row between the cousins Célèstine and he had formed the habit of dining each evening in Grasse, making as their excuse the fact that pressure of work would not allow them to leave the factory in time to dine at the château.

So the Comtesse's brave plan had come to nothing; lack of opportunity had prevented any repetition of the last stormy evening, and Fleur was secretly thankful at being spared a similar ordeal.

Besides, she had become convinced over the past few weeks that there could never be a second passionate scene with herself as the predominating influence; Alain's absorption with Célèstine was ample evidence that he was now regretting the impulse that had driven him to marry a girl he had never seen.

Almost without thought, her feet had carried her in the right direction and a shout of welcome from nearby workers jolted her out of her reverie.

Instantly, her face lit up and she returned their greetings happily, completely at ease with her new friends.

She spent a happy hour wandering along the rows of bushes talking to the pickers whose nimble fingers never once stopped in their task of gathering the sweet-smelling petals while at the same time, in halting English and with many uproarious attempts to mime, they managed to convey to her up-to-date news of their families.

As the sun rose higher, generating molten heat, she felt the first twinges of a headache. Gradually the rows emptied of pickers as they departed for the break they took each afternoon, to return later when the sun's rays were not so fierce and they were able to work in comfort.

Fleur followed in their wake, her headache now too marked to be ignored, and accepted thankfully an invitation from Maman Rouge to share the meal they brought with them each day to the fields.

She declined food, for her stomach revolted most decisively against sharing the wedges of bread, strong cheese and onion that were offered, but she eagerly accepted the cup of strong coffee that was handed to her. As she sipped at it, Maman Rouge scrutinized her white face and rebuked her with much concern for not having brought a hat.

"Our sun is much stronger than your weak English variety, Madame la Comtesse, and already you are looking pale! Jean-Paul!" she screeched suddenly at a cheeky-faced boy who was at that moment running past. "Go to your mother and ask if Madame might borrow her new sunbonnet. *Vite! Vite!* And tell her I sent you!"

"Oh, really, it isn't necessary!" Fleur protested, wondering at the back of her mind if she really did look such a wreck that everyone should be commenting about it. But Maman Rouge's dictate was reinforced by another of the group, a sweet-faced young girl whose large dark eyes had not left Fleur's face since she had joined the party. "Maman Rouge is right, *madame,* it would be a tragedy if you were to spoil such a beautiful complexion," she offered shyly.

The rough chorus of agreement that came from the men caused a tide of rich color to flood her cheeks and one man, older than the rest and therefore privileged, leaned forward to pass a teasing compliment.

"You are aptly name, Madame Fleur, for, if you will excuse my presumption, you are the favorite flower of all that grow around us. I named you 'English Rose,' but on second thoughts I have changed my mind. The English rose is attractive enough, but it cannot equal those of Bulgaria. Roses grown in the hilly Balkan country are the loveliest in the world; none can compare with them just as, in our opinion, none can compare with you, Madame la Comtesse. Now that Monsieur le Comte's experiments are quite finished we have two triumphs to celebrate tonight—the coming of the fairest flower of the family of Treville with the most subtle perfume ever devised by Maison Treville! Mmmm!" he bunched his fingers and lifted them to his lips in a smacking kiss. "What an achievement for Monsieur le Comte!"

So Alain's work was finished. Fleur did not doubt the old man's assertion, because on plantations, as in villages, secrets are kept only for as long as it takes one man to tell another. But she had not the heart to tell them that the perfume was not for her—that Célèstine's claim to it was far superior and of much longer duration than her own—and also she did not want to spoil the party that had been arranged for them that evening.

All at once, the row of laughing, expectant faces blurred into one with the sheet of blue sky and began wavering in front of her as if seen through a heat haze. The heavy perfume of the flowers, merged with the smell of strong cheese and garlic, began pressing down, depriving her of air so that she could not breathe.

Chattering voices escalated into a tremendous clamoring when, with a choking sigh, she slid from her seat and blackness descended upon her in an irresistible wave.

When she came to she was lying flat on a rough couch in one of the workers' huts. It was dim, cool and silent and for a moment she was bewildered by her unfamiliar surroundings. She struggled to sit up, but before she was upright Maman Rouge's kind, wrinkled face appeared above her head.

"Lie still for a moment longer, *mon*

enfant," she urged, "to give yourself time to recover."

Fleur sank back and admitted ruefully, "You were right to rebuke me, Maman Rouge. I must have a touch of sunstroke!"

"Indeed, yes." The old peasant nodded affirmation and showed signs of distress. "We ought to have warned you sooner about the strength of the sun upon an unprotected head. What Monsieur le Comte will say when he hears of our neglect I shudder to think. We deserve to be cursed for the idiots we all are!"

"Nonsense!" Fleur tried to sit up, but the effort brought on a wave of dizziness that caused her to sink back thankfully upon the bed.

Her voice surprised her by its weakness when she continued to try to soothe the old woman's fears. "It is entirely my own fault. I should have known better than to wander around bareheaded in this heat. When I've rested for a while, I'll make my way back to the château and no one will be any the wiser."

"*Mon Dieu!*" The old woman blanched at the thought. "That will never be allowed, Madame la Comtesse! One of the men must drive you back to the château! Bad enough that we allowed you to suffer because of our unthinking stupidity, but never must it be said that we were guilty of deliberate neglect! No, when you are able, you will be transported back home in one of the trucks."

Nothing Fleur said could budge her from this decision, and so it was that instead of creeping up to her room by a side door as she had planned, she was driven to the front of the house in a smoke-belching truck whose engine made so much noise that it aroused everyone in the château when it came up the drive.

The servants were the first to appear, but as the voluble driver made known to them the reason for his noisy appearance the Comtesse appeared at the head of the steps demanding an explanation.

One quick glance at Fleur's ashen face as she was helped out of the truck was enough to startle her into giving terse instructions, and before Fleur quite knew how it happened she was being tucked up in bed in her own blessedly cool room where shades were drawn against the hard light that by then was beating against her eyes, forcing a pain to throb through her head with the persistence of an insidious drum. The Comtesse uttered no word of reproach, but frowned anxiously when she gazed down into Fleur's pain-filled eyes.

"Try to rest, *ma petite*," she murmured. "The doctor has been sent for and should arrive very soon." When Fleur answered with a deep sigh and closed her eyes, she tiptoed from the room and closed the door softly behind her.

Fleur awoke much later completely free from pain. Gingerly, she raised her head from the pillow to test her reactions, and when the expected pain did not materialize she sank back with a smile of relief. For one dreadful moment she thought her stupid actions had jeopardized her chances of being present at the dinner party, and although she was not in the least looking forward to the event she would have been most upset on the Comtesse's account if all the weeks of preparation had been wasted.

Her bed gave a slight creak when she moved and she was startled when a voice carried a question across the dimness of the room.

"Are you awake?"

Her eyes sought the source of the voice and found Alain standing by the window, hardly visible against the screening drapes.

"Yes, thank you." She sounded small and

weak, like a child expecting a scolding. His voice had been austere but not unkind, and under the flimsy lace of her nightdress her heart began to pound. When he moved toward her she clasped her hands tightly and tried hard to control a fit of trembling when he sat down on the edge of the bed, so near that his presence overshadowed everything else in the room.

"They tell me you have not been looking well for weeks. I should have been told earlier." He frowned darkly. "This afternoon I gave instructions to the doctor that you are to have a complete checkup."

"The doctor has been?" The words tumbled out in a breathless rush.

He nodded. ".I brought him myself after receiving a telephone call from my mother telling me you were ill. When we arrived you were asleep, but he managed to make his examination without disturbing you and left instructions that you are to have a light diet and for a few days you are to stay out of the sun—especially at midday. You may get up whenever you feel like it, but you must do nothing strenuous."

His mouth relaxed into a smile so unexpected it took her breath away. " 'Mad dogs and Englishmen . . . !' " he quoted with a devastating lift of his eyebrow. "Even our tough, sun-baked pickers are wary of exposing their heads to the noon heat and yet you, I believe, do not hesitate! How can I guard you from the folly of your proud English independance? Will you give me your promise to be more careful in future?"

He sounded as if her answer really mattered, as if he intended staying there all day until he received her assurance that she would do as he asked.

She cleared her throat, but still the words came out huskily. "Very well, I promise."

For a few minutes there was silence, a pregnant, meaningful silence he made no attempt to break, and she became very conscious of his lean strength mere inches away from her. Her hands dropped to pull nervously at the silk coverlet and a restless movement of his resulted in their hands colliding.

When she tried to draw quickly away, her fingers were caught in his cool clasp and once more she thrilled to the terrifying ecstasy of his touch. It was the first time they had made physical contact since their wedding night when anger and contempt had motivated the hard passion that had driven him beyond control.

But anger held no sway over this brief

encounter, and in that moment she caught a glimpse of deep loneliness, a loneliness that was usually kept well hidden under his solitary, autocratic manner.

She suddenly felt his nearness too much. His touch was electrifying, sending a charge of high tension through her body and hitting her heart with a force that started the blood pounding in her ears. Her fingers fluttered in his, attempting an escape, but his grasp tightened.

"I—I feel well enough to get up now," she practically implored. "It must be almost time to begin getting dressed for the dinner party."

"There's no hurry," he told her coolly. "As it is some time since we talked together we might as well make the most of this opportunity."

She flinched from the memory of the last time they had exchanged words and tried to relax, but when his hand reached out and began to stroke her cheek she became startlingly alert.

"Your skin is velvet smooth," he murmured, "with the texture of a petal. Are you blushing? Your cheek feels hot beneath my hand."

His touch was so gentle and his eyes so

confusingly tender she could not draw away. His cool fingers were caressing not only her flushed face but also her wretched, troubled heart, and for the first time in weeks she began to feel completely at peace.

"You can be so understanding when you want to be, Alain," she whispered against his hand as it feathered against her mouth.

Her action surprised him. For a second his hand was still, then it descended with meaning to grip her shoulder. "Don't tease me, Fleur," he warned. "I am not a boy who can be tormented and then told to run away and play!"

His words underlined his deep mistrust of her and her heart jolted against her ribs. For some reason he had become approachable, but the balance of his emotions was so fine that one unthinking remark could upset his equilibrium and chase him back into his brooding shell.

Carefully, her eyes wet with tears, she whispered, "I am your wife, Alain!"

His fingers tightened on her shoulders with a strength that threatened to paralyze all feeling, but she gladly withstood the pain rather than destroy the fragile, unbelievable moment.

"Fleur!" Her name was crushed out from

between tightly compressed lips. With a small murmur of surrender she swayed toward him. His hands were reaching out to draw her closer when a tap sounded on the door and the Comtesse's voice cut through the tender ribbon of emotion.

"Well, *ma petite,* and how are you feeling now?" Her bird-bright eyes swept from Fleur's flushed face toward Alain, who had stood up as soon as his mother entered the room and was now a couple of paces away from the bed, his features a composed mask.

The Comtesse, always alert to the chance of furthering her cause, nodded meaningfully at Fleur before asking slyly, "May Louis come in? The poor boy has been distracted with worry since I told him of your mishap and he is blaming himself terribly for not taking more care of you. He will not rest until he has seen with his own eyes that you are quite recovered!"

When Alain's face darkened at the sound of Louis's name, Fleur sank back on her pillows with desolation in her heart. The Comtesse's well-meant interference had torn the flimsy fabric of understanding into a thousand pieces and she doubted if she would ever be allowed so close to Alain again.

Struggling to overcome her misery, she nodded and told the Comtesse, "Yes, of course, please tell him to come in." Then she closed her eyes to shut out the sight of Alain's rigid back as he strode, unspeaking, from the room.

AN HOUR LATER, composed and outwardly calm, Fleur began preparing for the evening ahead. The huge closet that had shown up her scanty possessions was no longer empty; days before, the clothes Alain had promised her had arrived and she now had a choice of outfit for every conceivable occasion.

But, as with the jewelry, their possession gave her no pleasure.

Size, fit and color were all perfect, carefully chosen by someone to whom explicit directions must have been given, but if it were not that the occasion was a grand one that called for a high standard of grooming she would have chosen to wear one of the dresses so lovingly stitched by her mother.

She stood undecided before the racks of clothes, trying to decide which dress to wear, and finally she picked a silk taffeta gown in a shade of pink that reminded her of the thrust of a tightly packed rosebud newly emerged from its protective boll. She laid it on the bed ready to step into after she had finished applying her makeup.

She had already bathed, so she crossed over to her dressing table and began coaxing her gleaming hair into heavy coils on top of her head, a style that added a regal dignity to her naturally graceful carriage. A touch of mascara to darken her lashes and the merest trace of pale pink lipstick and she was ready for the dress.

It whispered as she lifted it from the bed, and again when she stepped into it to zip it fastened. As she walked across the floor the sound intensified, a rustling and sighing that might have come from a despairing ghost always just one step behind her. Alain had mentioned in England that he liked her to wear taffeta because he had said being able to hear her movements compensated a little for not being able to see her, so it was not surprising that most of the evening dresses he had ordered were made of the same rich material and underskirts of taffeta had been included for wear with the shorter dresses.

She stood back from the mirror to judge the finished effect and wondered at the elegance money could achieve. The bodice of the dress was a pink shell above which her white shoulders rose satin-smooth; from her slender waist the skirt ran straight, following the line of her slim body, and stopped just short of the delicate cobweb of silver straps that formed an excuse for sandals. She bit her lip and frowned at her reflection. Her mouth still betrayed a tormented quiver that must not be allowed to be seen; her eyes echoed a sadness that was sure to excite comment from a company expecting to meet a radiant bride of a few weeks; and dark smudges under her eyes imparted an expression of fragile melancholy to her wan face. She was reaching for her makeup when a tap at the door caused her to brace instinctively. She turned toward the sound and reacted just in time to remove a pair of discarded shoes that lay directly in Alain's path as he walked unsuspectingly toward her. He stopped, his head tilted, and she knew he had heard the rustle of her dress when she moved.

"Fleur?" he clipped, his eyes roving the room, waiting for the answer that would pinpoint her presence.

"I'm here," she answered, her eyes assessing him gravely, wondering at the control that enabled him to suppress all the anger that burned within him.

For a brief moment he hesitated, then he

held out his hand to offer her the object he was holding.

Abruptly, he commanded, "Tonight, I wish you to wear this perfume. It is my new creation, the one that has kept me busy these past weeks. I hope you will like it."

Surprise overwhelmed her as she took the proffered glass vial. This was the perfume Célèstine coveted so much—why was he offering to give it to her?

She felt her question was answered when he went on coldly, "Most of the guests invited here this evening are competitors as well as friends. They will all have heard rumors of a new perfume from Maison Treville and I thought this an appropriate occasion to introduce both my new acquisitions."

"I understand," she answered mechanically, subduing the wave of hope that had led her mistakenly to believe he had chosen her particularly to be the one to introduce the perfume.

As the Comte de Treville he had a position to live up to, family honor to maintain, and that alone was reason enough for his decision even though afterward, once the proprieties had been seen by his friends to have been observed, the perfume would be handed over to its rightful owner.

She started violently when he stepped closer. "I shall put it on for you," he stated, so coldly matter-of-fact she could have believed she had dreamed the tenderness of an hour ago. She wanted to stammer a refusal, but he was already removing the vial from her nerveless fingers and unscrewing the stopper.

"First—" he took the stopper with its attached applicator and stroked it across her wrists "—it is applied to the wrists. Then to the crook of the elbow." His fingers burned her skin as he progressed up her arm. "Next, the throat."

His impersonal fingers started a pulse beating like a wild thing, and when he transferred his attention to her uncovered shoulders she had to battle hard to suppress tremors from running through her body. "A touch here—" his voice was beginning to sound constrained "—and a little on the upper lip is all that is needed."

He released her and stepped back, completely withdrawn.

The warmth of her body generated a cloud of fragrance such as she had never before enjoyed and she drew in a deep breath as the beautiful smell filled the room.

"Do you like it?" he questioned tentatively.

"Oh, yes!" She twirled around so that the

smell wafted about her, and breathed in deeply. "Lily of the Valley. . . . It reminds me of home, of the woods in springtime, of the garden after a shower of rain when the scent is so heavy and so glorious one feels enfolded in a mist of magic. Yes, it really does remind me of home!"

Ignoring her delight, he warned, "Never apply perfume behind the ears or on the nape of the neck, or its fragrance will simply float off behind you. Perfume, properly used, can work wonders. There is no more innocent or delicate means of self-expression, and by its use a woman's very soul, her spiritual atmosphere, can be infused around her in an unmistakable cloud of fragrance. It is not merely a cosmetic, but an essential aid for all women who wish to be more alluring and enticing to men."

She stared at him. If a perfume, to him, was such a personalized thing, how could he bear to allow her to wear one he had created especially for another woman—a woman who, both physically and spiritually, was her own direct opposite? Suddenly she felt she could not bear it.

Her tangled emotions, together with the slight weakness she still felt, combined to create within her a feeling of deep depression. If there had been time, she would have run to wash off the perfume she now felt was alien. Highly fastidious, she felt degraded, as if forced by circumstances to wear another woman's clothes, and the idea was abhorrent to her.

Her distaste was evident in her voice when she answered flatly, "You make it sound like a love philter, a bait with which to hypnotize the unsuspecting male! According to what you have just said, the relationship between perfume and personality is essential, but if this is so, the psychological side of your art requires more study, Alain! I have no wish to wear a perfume devised solely to stir men's emotions and I'll be obliged if you will hand the rest of it to the person for whom it was originally intended. Certainly I have no intention of ever using it again!"

His eyebrows drew together in a straight black line. All his aristocratic pride was evident in the haughty lift of his chin and in the flare of his narrow nostrils when he answered her in just two terse sentences.

"As you wish! Please be ready in five minutes to greet our guests!"

When he had left the room, she stood for a

moment, undecided; then a quick upsurge of hurt helped her to make up her mind. She grabbed the vial of perfume from the dressing table where Alain had left it and ran quickly to the door and out into the passageway. Célèstine's room was on the same floor as her own, and when she reached it she did not wait to knock but hurried straight inside before her courage could desert her. She was determined the perfume should be turned over to its rightful owner and the sooner the better. Although it was necessary to pretend, for the sake of Alain's friends, Célèstine had to be made aware that the farce was being played for one evening only.

But the room was empty. Célèstine had obviously just left, because her possessions were scattered all around the room and there was a mess on the dressing table that the maid had not had time to clean up.

Fleur's nose wrinkled with disgust as she stepped over discarded clothes to reach the dressing table where a pile of screwed-up tissues and other trivia betrayed Célèstine's untidy habits. Quickly, she cleared a space and left the vial where it could not fail to be noticed, then she hurried out of the room and went downstairs to Alain and the waiting Comtesse.

THE FIRST GUESTS were announced just as she reached Alain's side, and for the next hour she was fully occupied trying to memorize the many names and faces presented to her. Elegantly dressed women escorted by distinguished-looking men filed past to be introduced, all displaying a natural curiosity that was quickly replaced by genuine liking as Fleur's shy diffidence was communicated to them.

The men, especially, were not slow to voice their admiration and Alain's features grew slightly less bleak as the introductions continued until, by the time they were seated at the dinner table, his attitude toward her showed signs of thawing. She knew, of course, that the change was purely for the benefit of his friends, but basking in the warmth of his approval was a heady sensation that brought the sparkle back to her eyes and an upward tilt to her drooping mouth.

Célèstine, much to her own chagrin, had

been placed too far down the table to take part in Alain's conversation, and she had to be content with glowering every now and then at Fleur and Louis who were in her direct line of vision.

But afterward, when dinner was over and the guests were circulating or sitting in groups around the room, she made a beeline for Alain, who was in the center of a group of local businessmen, all extolling praises of the new perfume.

Fleur found it amusing to be the focal point of so many inquisitive noses, and she almost giggled aloud when Monsieur Devereux, a rival manufacturer, took hold of her arm and began projecting his nose along its entire length, sniffing deeply.

"Ah!" He meditated for a second. "A sweet, fresh top note!"

Then he challenged Alain, "But to obtain that perfect match to the flower's true fragrance, you have added bergamot, verbena, lemon and . . . ?"

"And . . . ?" Alain retorted.

At his cryptic reply Monsieur Devereux looked almost apoplectic, and seeing Fleur's look of bewilderment Monsieur des Essalts, another of the party, offered an explanation.

"Devereux prides himself on being an expert 'smeller,' Comtesse, and refuses to admit himself beaten by the balance of ingredients your husband has used in his latest creation. A perfume expert is expected to be able to detect the finest shades of odors, to name the various ingredients used, and to say whether it is wholly natural, wholly synthetic, or partly one and partly the other, but Alain's skillful blending is so perfectly balanced that we experts are all baffled."

As Fleur acknowledged this tribute to Alain's talent she felt a deep thankfulness that he had retained the skill for which he was renowned. She was just about to thank Monsieur des Essalts for his ungrudging praise when Célèstine's voice cut into the conversation.

"And have you decided yet what name is to be given to the perfume, Alain?" The question rang out like a challenge, but he seemed unperturbed by the angry undertone projected into her words.

"Yes, I have decided," he answered smoothly. "The name is, of course, 'Lily of the Valley.' "

Amid the clamor of approval no one but Fleur saw the flash of chagrin that chased across Célèstine's proud face. The perfume was Célèstine's, blended and created only for her, and the naming of it could only represent a slight to her.

Monsieur des Essalts' next words came as something of a shock.

"Ah," he said. " 'Lily of the Valley!' A most apt title, *mon ami,* you have captured your wife's beauty and personality faithfully within your new creation."

Fleur's heart missed a beat as dreadful doubts assailed her. With a sense of anticlimax, she heard Monsieur Devereux grudgingly admit, "Yes, indeed. Alain, you have not lost your blending skill, nor has your gift for matching perfume to subject diminished. No one could possibly doubt that the young Comtesse—" he bowed toward Fleur "—is the inspiration behind 'Lily of the Valley'; its soft, delicate, sweet floral complex matches her personality perfectly."

"I wonder if the young Comtesse knows our charming legend about this particular flower?" It was the turn of Monsieur des Essalts to recapture Fleur's attention. "One springtime long ago a young man, while walking through the woods near Paris, picked a sprig of lily of the valley to take to his love. In return for this fragrant gift, he received a kiss. And to this day, on the first of May, which is when the incident is said to have occurred, any *jeune fille* in Paris who is given this lovely flower must repay the donor with a kiss."

While the two men had been speaking, Fleur's eyes had gradually widened with growing alarm.

There was a question she had to ask and she forced it out huskily. "Thank you for your compliments, gentlemen, but would not this new perfume also suit the personality of others—Célèstine, for example?"

The immediate chorus of dissent that greeted her question verified her growing suspicion that she had badly misjudged Alain, and when Monsieur des Essalts took it upon himself to explain she listened with shocked dismay.

"You are right in one respect, Comtesse. There could be others with character and looks similar to your own who might wear this perfume successfully, but Célèstine? Never! Her type of beauty calls for the essences of the Orient, in fact, for the sultry, penetrating, jasmine-patchouli note that she is wearing at this very moment!"

Fleur could not bear to look at Alain, so

certain was she that his face would be registering grim satisfaction. He had not bothered to
deny her wild accusation; he had probably
considered it beneath his contempt and
unworthy of notice.

How she must have hurt him by her
rejection of his gift. Even if it had been meant
simply .as another payment of the debt he
considered he owed her, he had deserved to
have his generosity acknowledged.

Instead of which—she had given it away! A
wave of shamed remorse swept her. Franti-
cally she searched her mind for some way of
preventing her action from being found out
and with a flash of inspiration she recalled
Célèstine's empty room. Célèstine must have
already been downstairs when she had crept in
to deposit the bottle of perfume on her dressing table and as she had had no reason to
return upstairs since, the bottle must still
remain in her bedroom, undiscovered! Even as
the thought struck her her eyes swung toward
Célèstine, just in time to see her lift her shoulders in a disdainful shrug before moving away
from the men who were too engrossed in
talking shop to give her the attention her ego
demanded.

Fleur murmured an excuse and moved

discreetly away from the men, who were so intent upon their conversation they hardly noticed her departure. With her eyes firmly fixed upon the door by which she intended making her escape, she passed groups of chattering guests, smiling and nodding when they spoke but evading any attempt to delay her from her purpose.

Her hand was on the knob of the door, when Louis's deep voice sounded close to her ear and his detaining hand descended upon her arm.

"Where are you rushing off to in such a hurry?" he grinned, making no effort to hide his approval of the blush that exactly matched the pink rosebud color of her gown.

"I . . . I've left something in my room . . . a handkerchief. I was just slipping upstairs to get it," she stammered, the blush deepening as she forced out the lie.

"I'll ring for a servant," he insisted lazily, determined not to lose sight of her.

"Don't be silly," she answered crossly, fretting at the delay. "You know I've never been able to accustom myself to your habit of leaving everything to the servants, Louis, and I certainly wouldn't dream of asking one of them to undertake a task I can do myself in a matter of seconds."

His eyes suddenly narrowed. Ignoring her criticism, he bent to peer into her face and wondered aloud, "You look different tonight! I noticed it during dinner, but could not quite pin it down to any one thing. At first I thought it was your dress, but, becoming though it is, the cause of the change is not a material one. Now and then I watched a tremor pass your lips and saw you suppress it by digging in your pretty white teeth. Your hands shook when you lifted up your wine glass, and a couple of times when I spoke to you it seemed I was dragging you back to earth from out of some private dream world you were reluctant to abandon. What is it, Fleur? What inward upheaval has caused you to look upon the world with a madonna's eyes—full of tender, painful secrets?"

She recoiled from the notion that her unasked-for and unwanted love for Alain had become obvious to curious eyes. She wondered, with panic, if everyone present had the same awareness, then comforted herself with the thought that Louis was particularly acute. His perception was as great as Alain's, even more so—he could see! Fighting down the panic his words had caused, she made a brave attempt to appear unconcerned. She even managed to laugh a little when she drawled, "You have an inventive imagination, Louis, but it becomes overactive with too much wine."

The likeness between the cousins was never more marked than when their dignity was outraged, and when Louis's chin was arrogantly out-thrust she knew she had offended him. "Are you implying that I am drunk?" he demanded of her with a coldness akin to Alain's.

Her spirits sank. She had no wish to hurt his feelings, but she dared not allow him to probe further and, besides that, with each moment she was delayed her chances of recovering the vial grew slimmer. She had no choice but to offend him further.

"Not yet," she deliberately teased, "but you very soon will be and then Maman will become annoyed. Why don't you pay more attention to our young lady guests and allow your imagination to run riot in their direction? I'm sure they will be most gratified." Without waiting to hear his explosive reply, she slipped through the doorway and sped up the stairs toward Célèstine's bedroom.

A servant had tidied up the room, but otherwise everything remained as before. Lightheaded with relief, she tiptoed across to the dressing table and her hand was just about to close over the bottle when a voice cut through the silent room.

"Would you mind explaining what you are doing?"

She spun around to face Célèstine who was standing in the doorway, obviously having just followed her up the stairs.

The hard angry look she had worn all evening deepened as she waited, one foot tapping an impatient tattoo on the floor, for an answer.

"I'm sorry," Fleur gasped, "but I left something of mine here by mistake and I've come to collect it."

"Something of yours?" Célèstine walked up to the dressing table and her eyes grew stormy when they alighted upon the vial of perfume. "Why is that here in my room?" she demanded imperiously.

"I brought it just before dinner," Fleur admitted, knowing it was useless to prevaricate any longer. "I made a terrible mistake in thinking Alain had created it especially for you and although I knew I had to wear it this evening for the benefit of his friends, I wanted you to have what was left. However—" she drew in a deep breath and closed her eyes for a second as she relived the memory "—what I heard downstairs made me realize the terrible mistake I had made. The perfume is mine and I've come to take it back."

Célèstine expelled a hissing breath, her beautiful young face growing ugly, distorted with a rage she made no effort to conceal. "I will find it hard to forgive Alain for leading me to believe the perfume was mine, then waiting for an occasion such as this to play his diabolical trick!"

Fleur shrank back from the venom in her voice. "Are you saying he planned it deliberately, just to hurt you?" she questioned huskily.

"What else?" Célèstine flung back. "I should have known there was some under-handed reason for his decision to dispense with me in favor of a new assistant, but I never dreamed he meant to deceive me in such a way! For weeks I have hung around the distillery, bored to distraction but willing to be on hand in case he should need me, and what is my reward? A slap in the face from the inhuman Comte whose insufferable dignity will not allow him to rest until all slights have been avenged!"

"Do you mean," Fleur faltered, fastening

onto a ray of hope, "that all these weeks while you have been together at the distillery you have seen hardly anything of him?"

Célèstine's mouth twisted into a derisive sneer. "That is so, my dear, but that, too, was part of my punishment; he wanted revenge, to pay me back for imaginary wrongs! But do not deceive yourself that everything between us is ended. Come, stop pretending and begin to face facts! Why do you think he feels such revenge is necessary? Why would any man who is supposedly indifferent to a woman go to such lengths to hurt her?"

When Fleur flinched she smiled and continued in a satisfied purr, "We understand one another, Alain and I. Ours is a love-hate relationship that far outshines the wishy-washy emotion you English call love and, make no mistake about this, he will be drawn to my side whenever I call, however much you might appeal to his chivalry and his sense of responsibility. His mother can remind him as often as she wishes about his position and his duty toward you, but he is tied to me by bonds far stronger than bonds of marriage. He knows this, the Comtesse knows it, and now—you know it!"

Fleur nodded, hypnotized into believing by the force of conviction behind the words, and too dazed with hurt to deny the cruel statements.

How could she deny what she knew to be true? Alain's complex nature was such that he could derive savage satisfaction from hurting the one who was closest to him. She knew that from her own experience in England when for a few short weeks she had been the only one to bear the brunt of his displeasure. And then again, she had guessed right from the beginning that there was more between Célèstine and himself than was ever allowed to show on the surface.

Still struggling with chaotic thoughts, she straightened and without speaking made to leave.

Célèstine watched her, a lazy, feline smile playing about her lips, and when she had almost reached the door she mockingly questioned, "What about your perfume? Isn't that what you came for?"

Fleur mustered a shred of dignity and turned to answer quietly.

"Thank you, but I should be glad if you would dispose of it for me. I never want to wear it again."

When Fleur left the room Célèstine's smile disappeared. Sounds from downstairs told her that guests were beginning to leave, so she decided against returning to the party. Her eyes fell upon the vial of perfume and she picked it up and looked at it long and thoughtfully, then with a slow smile she made her way to the bathroom to run her bath.

Fleur, too, heard the sound of departing guests, but nothing could have persuaded her to face the prolonged goodbyes she knew she could expect if she returned to speed them on their way.

Knowing the family would make some apology for her absence, she went straight to her room and closed the door with a feeling of relief. Here, she had no need to pretend that all was well between Alain and herself; the strain of behaving all evening like a devoted and cherished wife had been greater than she had realized.

Her hands shook as she prepared for bed and it was much later as she lay, unable to sleep, that she forced herself to review the conversation between Célèstine and herself. Nagging doubts, subdued until then by Célèstine's forceful arguments, were allowed space in her mind and her just nature rebelled against taking Célèstine's word without first seeking confirmation from Alain. He was too honest, she assured herself inwardly, to carry on an alliance with Célèstine while still married to herself.

He had taken his marriage vows with an impressive sincerity that still lingered in her mind, making it impossible for her to believe in his deceit. While he had made it quite plain before their marriage that he neither offered nor wanted love in return, she had nevertheless been made aware of his genuine regard and his unswerving resolve that she would never have cause to regret her decision to become his wife. She clung to these facts with desperation, forcing them to the forefront of her mind so that they might enable her to whip up sufficient courage to confront Alain with a request to either confirm or deny Célèstine's words.

It seemed a long time later that she heard him walk past her door on his way to his room. She would have confronted him there and then, but it was late and the questions she wanted to ask would sound better in the morning when she hoped she would be better able to control the emotional quiver in her voice.

Just then, a featherlight tap sounded on the door that connected her bedroom with the bathroom she shared with Alain. She was so startled that for a moment she remained very still, staring in the direction of the sound, but when it was not repeated she relaxed, telling herself it was the work of her overactive imagination. But the noise bothered her. She jumped out of bed, shrugged on her negligee, and walked over to the door. She hesitated for a moment, then turned the handle and walked inside.

Across the width of the floor speared a ray of light that came from Alain's partially open door. She wavered, but an undeniable compulsion drew her forward. Through the gap she could see into the interior of the room and the scene inside turned her limbs to stone and her heart to a hurt, quivering mass. As she watched, Célèstine, looking especially lovely in a dressing gown of stiff white brocade, its high, outstanding collar framing her face, rustled across to Alain and stood close to him for a moment without speaking before raising her arms to place them confidently around his neck.

For a moment he looked startled, as if her presence in his room was unexpected, but then his face was transformed by a look of such immense pleasure that Fleur knew she was looking at a man deeply in love. When his arms reached out to clasp Célèstine around the waist, Fleur lingered no longer. She withdrew from the scene, her ragged feelings unable to cope with more, and stepped backward into the darkness. But before she was out of earshot she heard Alain's deep voice murmuring with passionate feeling, "Oh, my heart's darling, how I've yearned to have you back in my arms!"

Sickened, and so hurt she could hardly swallow back the tears that constricted her throat, she stumbled back to her room, sank back on the bed, and stared with desolate eyes at the square of ceiling above her head, searching its empty surface for an answer to the problem that had suddenly become insoluble.

Chapter Ten

IT WAS NOT QUITE four o'clock the next morning when Fleur left the château. She crept downstairs, her shabby suitcase, packed with only those possessions she had brought with her from England, gripped tightly in her hand. In the solemn quiet of early morning the château was full of unexpected creaks and sudden small noises. A dozen times she halted in her tracks, in a sweat of fear, in case one of the sounds should herald the arrival of Alain demanding to know why she was opting out of fulfilling her end of their bargain.

The solid wooden doors swung open easily

in response to her touch, and once outside she stepped onto the grass and began to run along the length of the drive, never once allowing her steps to falter until the massive iron gates loomed into view and she knew there was no longer any danger of being seen from the house.

The road was deserted. She had no idea which direction she should take, only that she wanted to get to Nice where she knew she could board a plane for England—and home. So she took a wild guess and began walking in the opposite direction to Grasse, arguing to herself that as the town was inland and the château stood between it and the coast she must surely be going in the right direction. After traveling along what seemed miles of tree-lined road without coming across a sign-post or any person who might have directed her, her steps began to flag. Her suitcase felt like a ton weight and in her hurry to leave the château she had not stopped to consider the need for food.

Dinner the evening before had been the last meal she had eaten and the exercise of walking, together with the freshening effect of clear morning air, had combined to make her feel ravenously hungry.

She was just about to sit down for a rest when she heard behind her the chugging of a heavy motor.

Her first instinct was to hide, but then she reasoned that no one from the château would use such an obviously slow-moving form of transport with which to catch her up so she waited hopefully at the side of the road until the noise appeared in concrete form.

It was a tractor-driven wagon, piled with boxes of cut flowers, and her relief was tremendous when in answer to her one desperate word, "*Aéroport?*" the young driver nodded his understanding of her pleas for a lift and answered, "*Mais oui, mademoiselle!*"

She could have kissed his cheerful young face when he leaned to clear a space, then helped her onto the wagon. Her understanding of the local *patois* had improved enormously during her many talks with the pickers and she had no difficulty in understanding when he told her he was on his way to the flower market in Nice.

He seemed glad of her company, even though the noise of the tractor made conversation difficult, and when he took from his pocket a packet containing bread and cheese and offered to share it with her she accepted gladly.

Munching her slice of fresh bread—not long from the oven and spread liberally with pale, creamy butter—she sat high behind the lumbering tractor and watched the coastline draw nearer, feeling for the first time since her discovery of Alain's treachery a sense of peace entering her soul. She would soon be home, back with her loving parents and the friends she had missed so badly.

Wistfully, she wondered if the old Comtesse would miss her. She had not had time to write a note, her flight had been made on impulse, but she promised herself that as soon as she reached home she would write to her and try to explain, in a way that would cause her as little pain as possible.

Very soon, the tractor rumbled into the streets of Nice. The promenade and avenues were deserted, and only one or two flower sellers were setting up stalls in the market-place, preparatory to displaying their blooms. Fleur jumped from the wagon, thanked the young man for his help, then set off according to his directions to find a taxi that would take her to the airport. A sense of urgency was

beginning to make itself felt. About this time
of day the occupants of the château would be
beginning to stir, and she wanted to be well on
her way to England when her absence was
discovered.

With relief, she hailed a cruising taxi and
scrambled into it, giving the rapid instructions:
"*Aéroport, vite, s'il vous plâit!*" It was not
until she had been driven almost half the way
there that she realized her hands were shaking
and her heart was beating with hard, nervous
thumps.

As soon as they arrived at the airport she
paid off the taxi and hurried into the vast
reception area where, even at that early hour,
porters were rushing trolleys full of luggage
toward moving conveyor belts and people were
rushing to buy coffee, cigarettes and boxes of
freshly cut flowers as last-minute mementos,
as well as demanding all kinds of information
from the harassed staff.

Her fingers gripped her bag with unconscious apprehension as she approached the
counter and stated her requirements. "One
seat on the first available flight to London,
please," she stammered.

The official smiled reassuringly, thinking the
nervous timidity he saw in her face had its

origin in a fear of flying. "You will be quite safe, *mademoiselle,* no need to worry! Wait until your flight number is called, then go to the appropriate gate where a stewardess will be waiting to take you to the plane. You have plenty of time," he added swiftly when she clutched her ticket and looked ready to run. "Your plane is not due to leave for two hours yet!"

Two hours! Somehow she had not expected to be delayed. Her fevered mind had led her to imagine she would step out of the taxi and straight onto a plane that would whisk her away to England before any last-minute doubts could begin to cloud her mind. But two hours!

That was time enough for Alain to alert the police and half the countryside.

She wandered disconsolately into the airport lounge and found a corner seat partly obscured by a large potted palm. She sat down facing the plate-glass window that looked out onto the tarmac and prepared to wait, determined to keep her thoughts from straying to Alain and the scene that had precipitated her hurried departure.

At first it was not hard—the incoming and outgoing planes were fascinating to watch—but then as passengers disembarked it seemed each batch contained at least one tall, lithe figure whose arrogant profile caused her heart to lurch with sickening force, then subside into a terrified thumping when she realized she was jumping at shadows her tormented mind had fashioned into images of Alain.

A dozen times she looked at her watch, urging the hands forward to the appointed time, until at last over the metallic-sounding loudspeaker she heard her flight announced. She moved quickly toward the departure gate with her eyes fixed straight ahead and her mind so intensely set upon reaching it that she did not hear her name when it was called. She had just joined the end of the quickly forming line when a hand closed over her arm and a voice called out, "Fleur! Thank God I've found you!"

She spun around, her face ashen. "Louis!" Her tone implored him not to delay her as her fellow travelers began moving toward the waiting plane.

"Fleur, wait! I must speak with you!"

"Not now, Louis," she answered wildly. "I'll miss my plane. I'll write as soon as I reach home, I promise!"

She was almost through the gate when he caught hold of her again and swung her around to face him.

For the first time she noticed the signs of distress in his face. His hair was tousled by agitated fingers and he was breathing heavily as if fighting to overcome the aftermath of a strenuous sprint.

"Fleur, it's Maman, she's had some sort of an attack. The doctor is with her now, but she's been asking for you."

"*Maman?* Oh no!" Her shocked cry was drowned by the revving of powerful engines, but she did not give a second thought to the plane that was waiting on the runway. "Take me to her at once, Louis! Hurry!"

It was not until she was in the car, speeding along the miles that separated Nice from the château, that Louis was able to explain fully. In a matter-of-fact, steadily controlled voice that emphasized rather than hid his strong feelings, he told her, "She was found lying on the floor of your room by the maid when she took up your early-morning tea. We think she must have felt anxious about you—when you did not reappear last night Alain explained to the guests that you had had a touch of sunstroke that afternoon and that because you had not quite recovered from it you had retired early.

"His mother accepted the explanation, but she must have awakened earlier than usual and decided to find out for herself how you were feeling. She had tried to reach the bell to summon help, but before she could reach it she collapsed. Luckily, it must have happened less than half an hour before she was discovered, otherwise the consequences might have been much more serious. A stroke is serious at any time, of course, but at her age . . . ." He shrugged and left the sentence unfinished.

"How bad is she?" Fleur whispered.

"One side of her body is paralyzed, but the doctor is hopeful that with careful nursing this condition will improve. Her words, when she tried to speak, sounded gibberish to me, but Alain understood. She was speaking your name, asking for you, and the only way we could get her to rest was by telling her I was going to fetch you. Thank God I started my search at the airport, otherwise in another few minutes you would have been on your way to England!"

He was concentrating on his driving, but her distress was so intense it was communicated to him. He glanced around and was shocked by the horror he saw in her eyes.

"Fleur! For heaven's sake! You're surely not blaming yourself for Maman's collapse—you couldn't possibly have foreseen . . . ."

When she crumpled up in her seat and began to sob he cursed his own stupidity and drew in to the side of the road. Then, pulling her forward into his arms, he cradled her shaking body and tried to comfort her. But her remorse went too deep for mere words, and it was a long time before her storm of weeping had subsided enough to enable his words to penetrate.

"It was not your fault, do you hear!" He shook her. "The Comtesse is old—it was unfortunate and terribly distressing that it should have been your absence that triggered off the stroke, but it could have happened any time, Fleur. You must believe that!" In his agitation he shook her again, but she was stiff and unresponsive.

Impelled by compassion, he half lifted his hand to stroke her bright hair, but changed his mind, and with a grim look of maturity upon his strained features he decided to try to arouse her from her numbness by appealing to her for help.

"I do not intend to ask questions, Fleur," he told her quietly, "but as it is obvious that the situation between yourself and Alain is much worse than we thought, I must ask you a favor." She did not stir, but he was sure he had her attention, so he carried on. "Will you stay at the château? Maman needs a woman, someone who loves and understands her as you do. The servants are devoted, but they are not the same as family, as I am sure you will agree. And Fleur. . . ." She looked up when he hesitated, wondering what it was he found so hard to say, and faint color stained her cheeks when he went on, "I feel I must ask this of you, both for my aunt's sake and for Alain's. Although both he and his mother need you desperately, it is quite plain that after your flight from him today his pride would never allow him to ask for your help."

Her color receded, leaving her deathly white.

"He must hate me for what I have done to his mother," she whispered, her blue eyes pools of agonized remorse. "And why should he want me around when he has Célèstine?"

"She packed her bags and left for Paris this morning," he answered flatly.

Hardly able to believe it, she faltered, "Does Alain know?"

"Presumably, since it was he who told me," he shrugged. "It seems they discussed the possibility of the trip last night, and this morning, even though she was told of the Comtesse's illness, Célèstine saw no reason to change her mind—she hates sickrooms, so she has gone, bag and baggage, and good riddance!" he flared contemptuously.

For long seconds they were wrapped in silent thought: Louis hoping desperately that his plea would penetrate her numbed senses and Fleur fighting with the devastating knowledge that she had almost caused the death of the old lady she loved. Finally, Louis broke the silence.

"Well, what do you intend to do? There is no question of your being forced into a decision, but if you feel you cannot stay it might be less painful for Maman if you leave now without seeing her at all. Believe me, *ma petite*, if that is what you decide I will understand. Just say the word and I will drive you straight back to the airport."

He was pretending she had a choice, but she knew she had none. Even if she had not come to love the Comtesse as much as she did, her strong sense of duty would not have allowed her to desert her in her hour of need. But she had Alain to face.

Louis never guessed the effort it cost her to whisper, "Please drive on, Louis. Of course I must stay."

She went straight up to the Comtesse's room when she reached the château. The doctor had left, but a nurse was in attendance upon the old lady whose frail body barely disturbed the surface of the silk coverlet that was spread like a bright wave of mimosa across her bed.

Fleur tiptoed across the carpet, and was shocked to see how small and withered the Comtesse had become. Her face was etched like a delicate porcelain carving against the pristine pillows; her hands, with blue veins showing prominent through almost transparent skin, were still, their lifelessness curiously emphasized by the absence of the many rings she usually wore. When the nurse held up her hand, warning her not to speak, her apron crackled and the crisp sound split the silence of the room with the impact of clashing cymbals.

There was an almost imperceptible movement from the bed, then a low moan, and the Comtesse opened her eyes just as Fleur's concened face appeared above her head. Her drug-clouded eyes brightened, and her lips moved to speak, but the effort was too much and with a sigh she slipped back into unconsciousness—but with a small, secret smile tugging at the corner of her mouth.

The nurse motioned Fleur out of the room and when she obeyed she followe her into the passageway.

"She knew you, *madame*, and she is now content. She will not awaken again until the sedative has worn off, so if you take my advice, you will sleep yourself for an hour or two. You look as if you need it," she concluded with a keen professional look at Fleur's wan face and unsteady mouth.

Fleur thanked her and agreed to follow her suggestion, but when she was back in her own room she knew sleep would be impossible. She had one more upsetting duty to perform before she could even hope to rest. She washed away all traces of tears and changed into a fresh dress before going downstairs in search of Alain.

He was alone in the library, sitting in a deep leather armchair placed in front of the window so that a stream of sunlight played on his dark head with the directness of a silver-bladed lance.

Her cotton dress did not betray her with a whisper as she glided through the partially open door, and when her eyes fell upon his hands, clenching and unclenching as he wrestled with solitary thoughts, her heart sank.

"Alain!" Although she tried to project her voice his name sounded like a frightened whisper, but she knew he had heard when he froze to attention, his restless hands immediately still. "Alain," she trembled as she walked toward him, "I'm so terribly sorry!"

He stood up and towered over her. "You have seen her?"

"Yes," she choked. "She knew me . . . she smiled." She could not go on.

His grim mouth relaxed, but not enough to form a smile. He moved, an uncertain, uncharted movement that projected his foot against the leg of a chair, sending him slightly off balance. She darted forward to help him, but he righted himself immediately and groped outward with his hands, seeking the back of his chair. Fleur was shocked. It was the first time he had ever shown any lack of confidence; he seemed stripped of all the arrogant assurance that so annoyed Louis but that to her had symbolized his complete independence of everyone around him.

She was not allowed time to wonder at the change in him. Aloofly, as if aware he had betrayed a weakness, he asked, "Will you please sit down, Fleur? I think it is time we discussed our future."

Her heart turned over when he ran his fingers through his hair with a movement so dispirited, so weary, it seemed to indicate that all his brave battles had been lost.

Suddenly it seemed terribly important that he should know how bitterly she regretted her actions. Her heart was full of the words she wanted to say, but all she managed to force through her trembling lips was the inadequate sentence: "I'm sorry, Alain, so very sorry."

He went white to the mouth. "I'm sorry, too, Fleur, sorry I talked you into a marriage that has brought nothing but regrets. I made a dreadful mistake; I only wish it were possible to turn back the clock so that you might be spared more heartbreak."

The meaning behind his words brought staggering pain.

He had no need to go on, no need to spell out his yearning for Célèstine when she had already heard and witnessed with her own eyes the intensity of the love he felt for her. She had to stop him from saying any more, stop him before her pitiful defenses crumbled and she embarrassed him still further by pleading with him not to send her away.

"Don't worry about me, Alain. I'll stay for a while until your mother recovers, but afterward . . . ."

"Thank you, it is good of you to even consider doing so, in the circumstances," he replied gravely.

"I know what your presence here means to her, so I cannot try to dissuade you from staying, but—" his face wavered in a gray mist as he considered his next words carefully before continuing in a controlled voice that contained neither apology or remorse "—do you think you will find your stay easier if I tell you I intend going away for a while?"

"Probably!" Pride made her answer just one word.

He stood up to walk a few paces away, turning his back toward her. "Aren't you

interested enough even to ask where?" he
demanded with sudden savagery.

Again, it was just as well her answer needed
only one word, because it was all she was
capable of uttering. Tense and unhesitantly,
she answered him.

"No!"

Then she ran from the room as if it
contained all the devils in hell. She had no need
to ask where. Célèstine was in Paris, so where
else would he be going but there?

Chapter Eleven

FLEUR WAS PUSHING the Comtesse's wheelchair along the path that wound its way
through the grounds of the château. It was
October, almost two months since the
Comtesse's stroke and Alain's desertion, which
had followed just a short week later, but the
sun was shining upon a countryside profuse
with flowers; only the scent had changed from
that of roses and mimosa to the even headier
fragrance of geranium and wild mint. Fleur
stopped and carefully positioned the wheelchair so that fingers of shade cast by tall
cypress trees protected the Comtesse from the

sun, then she sat down on a convenient garden seat facing her.

"Are you comfortable, Maman? Would you like a cushion behind your head?"

The Comtesse smiled up into her anxious face and chided gently, "Stop hovering, child! I am almost completely recovered, the doctor himself has assured you of this, and yet still you insist upon cosseting me as if I were made of some insubstantial substance the sun's rays might melt. I insist you sit down and stop fussing."

The words were gently said, but meant to be obeyed, so Fleur smiled and relaxed in her seat, comforted by the knowledge that what the Comtesse had just said was true: except for being still a little unsteady on her feet, and the fact that she now grew tired easily, she had made a marvelous recovery. For weeks Fleur had watched over her, hardly leaving her side by night or day, until the doctor had insisted upon her relaxing her vigil for the sake of her own health and his peace of mind. But she had found it impossible to take his advice. Constantly, she had been drawn back to the Comtesse's side, anticipating her every need, and finally she had been rewarded by a lightening of the tremendous load of guilt that burdened her mind when as each day passed she saw signs of progressive improvement.

Alain's absence hovered like a giant question mark between them. The Comtesse had never once questioned her about the events that had led up to her flight from the château. It was as if she wished to erase the incident from her mind, to pretend it had never happened, and Fleur was content to have it so because she knew the old lady was not yet well enough to withstand the upset of having the painful subject reopened. It would have to be discussed, of course. Sooner or later Alain would have to make known his attachment to Célèstine, but his absence lessened the urgency of a decision and each day he remained away extended the Comtesse's chances of being well enough to weather the shock when it came.

The Comtesse settled back in her chair and looked thoughtfully across to Fleur. "Did you know I had spoken to Alain on the telephone last night?" she inquired, her knowledgeable old eyes seeming capable of reading thoughts.

Fleur gave a visible start and lifted her hand involuntarily to her cheeks to hide the rush of burning color. She knew that during his absence he had been in constant touch with his mother by telephone, but not once had he asked to speak to her and pride had prevented her from asking the Comtesse for news of him.

"No," she managed to answer, "I did not know. How is he?"

Cautiously, obviously wary in case an unthinking word should cause distress, the Comtesse told her, "He sounded in surprisingly good spirits; in fact, his voice was so confident and so full of vigor I could have believed I was speaking to the man he used to be, the son I thought was lost to me forever." She wiped away a vagrant tear, then, as if determined not to succumb to the weakness of self-pity, she took a deep breath and spoke with asperity. "He would not speak of himself. Even when I tried to insist upon knowing when he would be returning home all he did was tease me by saying that he preferred that his homecoming should come as a surprise but that when he did come home he would have some very special news for me that he wished to deliver in person. It is most annoying of him to persist with this secrecy," she frowned. "Why won't he even tell me where he is staying? What possible reason can he have for wanting to keep us in ignorance of his whereabouts?"

Fleur did not reply. It was agony to think of

him in Paris with Célèstine. Many times during the past weeks she had wakened from her sleep imagining his arms were around her, hearing in her dreams his husky voice whispering wonderful, passionate phrases and feeling for a fleeting, drowsy second a delirious happiness as she teetered once again on the threshold of the heaven she had been introduced to one rapturous night when the scent of roses had drifted through the open window to add extra sweetness to those precious hours. She wondered if he, too, remembered.

But when the Comtesse's words returned to mock her she knew she was grasping at straws, dreaming impossible dreams. He had sounded in surprisingly good spirits, she said—confident and full of vigor. If Célèstine had wrought such a wonderful change in him she deserved to be congratulated. Not even Maman, with her built-in resistance to Célèstine's charms, would be able to speak disapprovingly of the woman who had restored her son to her, and still less would she find it possible to object to their alliance once Alain made it plain how much his future happiness relied upon having her by his side.

She stood up quickly, unable to bear the agony of such thoughts, and forced back an onrush of tears as she comforted the old lady. "I'm certain Alain will not keep you in suspense much longer, Maman, and meanwhile you must stop worrying. Think how disappointed he will be if he should return home to find you too ill and upset to hear his news! Come now—" she exerted gentle pressure upon the Comtesse's shoulders "—lean back and close your eyes. It is time for your nap."

She sat beside the wheelchair for ten minutes until she was sure the Comtesse was asleep, then she tiptoed along the path until she reached a favorite spot that gave a wonderful panoramic view of the plantations and the surrounding countryside. Beneath the spot where she sat the ground fell away, then rose in the distance in waves of vivid red, shaded here and there by tones of pink. Massed geranium petals, heavy with a perfume so potent it drugged the senses and with a beauty so indescribable that to gaze too long was to induce a hypnotic state bordering almost upon stupor.

It was here Louis found her half an hour later. It was quite some seconds before she became aware of him standing looking down at her, and when she eventually did her pensive face lightened with a smile of welcome.

"Why, Louis, how unusual to see you at this time of day! Maman was remarking only this morning how little we see of you these days. Suddenly you seem to have become a dedicated businessman!"

He did not respond with a smile to her teasing, and when he dropped down beside her and said gravely, "Fleur, I must talk to you," her eyes widened with foreboding. She twisted around to send a panic-striken look toward the wheelchair, but he shook his head and reassured her, "She's perfectly all right. When I passed her she was sleeping soundly."

She relaxed. "Then what is it, Louis? What have we to discuss that makes you look so serious?"

But now the opportunity he had sought was upon him he seemed to be having difficulty in finding words. She waited patiently, her eyes puzzled, until he had sorted out his thoughts, then stiffened with shock when he abruptly jerked out, "Is everything over between you and Alain?"

The geranium red mass behind her was no brighter than the color in her cheeks when she whispered, "You have no right to ask me that, Louis."

Her answer snapped the tight rein on the

feelings he had sought to contain and with sudden anger he turned on her. "But I do have that right, Fleur; no one has more right! For weeks I have watched you slowly dying inside while you wait for a word or a sign from the man whose neglect of you absolves him of all rights as a husband! Each day your eyes have grown a little sadder, your lovely face a little less serene until now you are a silent little shadow that creeps around the château with a heart that is heavy with remorse and a spirit too depressed to recognize the love I have found impossible to conceal. I love you, Fleur!"

His hands fastened upon her shoulders as if impelled to shake the dazed incomprehension from her eyes. "Come away with me—now, today—and I swear I will spend my whole life making up to you for Alain's devilish treatment!"

When he pulled her forward, intent upon kissing her trembling mouth, her numbed senses revived. With every bit of strength she possessed she pushed against him so that he had to let her go.

"How could you, Louis!" she panted, so shaken she had to tense every muscle for control. "How could you betray not only my friendship but also your family's trust! Have you no thought for Maman's feelings? I know there is little accord between yourself and Alain, but surely he has done nothing to deserve such treachery from you. I am Alain's wife, Louis! You might forget that fact—and so might he—but I never shall!"

When her voice broke on a heartbroken sob, his shoulders sagged. For a while there was silence between them, then hesitantly he spoke.

"I tried to fight it, Fleur. I am not so entirely without conscience that I found it easy to plan to steal the wife of a man who is blind. If Alain still had his sight I would not have found it necessary these past weeks to work myself almost to a standstill in an effort to keep my mind off loving you. But he does not deserve such consideration! He left you to cope alone with Maman and went off to pursue his own interest without a thought for either of you. How can you defend him? Surely you can't still have a regard for him?"

"Would you have me hate him simply because he cannot return my love?" she asked simply.

"Most of the women I know would do just that!" he bit out in return.

She winced for him.

"Then I don't wonder you are so disillusioned, Louis."

"*Mon Dieu!*" He turned away with a defeated shrug. "I should have known better than to expect you to return my love. Alain is even more fortunate than I thought." He thrust his hands into his pockets and kicked moodily at a stone. "I suppose I now have no alternative but to leave the château."

"No, Louis, you can't do that! What about Maman? How can you even think of deserting her when her health is so precarious? You must stay, for her sake and also for the sake of the business. Who will make the necessary decisions if both you and Alain are absent?"

"*Alain! Alain!* Always your thoughts are for him!"

He threw his arms wide in a furious Gallic gesture, amazed that she should be worrying about the man who alone was responsible for her own heartbreak. He was so angry on her behalf she saw no choice but to make him fully aware of the situation between Alain and herself.

Steadily, with her emotions firmly under control, she told him, "It is I who will be leaving the château. When Alain returns he will be bringing Célèstine to stay . . . permanently."

He stared back at her, surprised and shocked. "It can't be true! Are you sure of this?" he questioned sharply, hardly needing to doubt her words when he glimpsed the agony that darkened her deep blue eyes to purple.

"Yes, quite sure." But when she saw a flash of renewed hope lighten his eyes she had to disillusion him. "But that makes no difference to my feelings toward you, Louis." She swallowed hard, and when she again began to speak her voice had descended to a whisper. "I shall never love anyone but Alain, never." Her hand went to the little blue charm she always wore around her neck and he knew, with quick insight, that she was thinking of the inscription that might have been penned exclusively for herself and Alain. "Together but always apart!"

Marriage vows bound them, but nothing, it seemed, would ever bridge the gulf that kept them apart. Her courage made him feel both ashamed and dejected. He was no scoundrel, but over the years an innate selfishness had been allowed to sway his character until he had become accustomed to taking for granted that whatever he wanted he must have—regardless of the cost. Dull color ran under his skin as for the first time he saw himself as he must appear in her eyes, and the picture was not a pleasant one. Discovering himself capable of shame was an experience he found hard to digest and his distaste was reflected in his voice when finally he came to a decision.

"Very well, I'll stay, but only because you ask it of me. *Le bon Dieu* knows I'm no martyr, but if you think my presence here will help then I cannot go." He spun on his heel and walked away, his back rigid with disapproval of his own uncharacteristic benevolence, then he hesitated and turned back toward her.

"Fleur!"

"Yes, Louis?" She trembled, not far from tears.

"I'm sorry if what I said hurt you. Can you forgive me?"

She recognized this as his way of saying the subject was now closed, never to be reopened or referred to again, and her generous heart opened to accept his plea. Her smile was like sun shining through clouds when she answered.

"Your friendship will always be very dear to me, Louis, I should hate to lose it. There is nothing to forgive."

It TOOK GREAT EFFORT to begin dressing for dinner that evening. The day had contained too much worry, too much emotion, and when she walked across to the closet to choose a dress Fleur's eyes were immediately drawn to a restful smoke-gray chiffon with a demure white collar that seemed to match precisely her mood of the moment.

The flimsy fabric moved silently around her as she walked, floating outward on each suspicion of a breeze, then wafting gently back without any betraying whisper to caress her slender ankles. She brushed her hair until it shone, but lethargy held her in its grip and instead of piling it on top of her head she left it to hang loosely down to her shoulders.

Somewhere downstairs there were sounds of unusual activity. A car door banged twice, voices echoed in the hall, then the footsteps began to ascend the stairs—eager, vital steps that spelled out the owner's impatience to arrive at his destination. When they came to a halt outside in the passageway her nerves began to pull. With a suddenly dry mouth she stared across at the door, willing whoever it was who hesitated outside to walk in and put her out of her misery.

The draught from the opening door caught

her dress and swirled it around her so that she looked enchantingly ethereal, like some fey creature caught up in a gray mist. Completely immobile, she waited, then released her breath in a sigh when Alain's tall figure walked into the room.

Hungrily, she watched him as he advanced toward her. Dark glasses screened his eyes, but through the misted glass they caught and held hers in a look so intense it would not be broken. An unaccountable shyness made her blush scarlet, and when he stopped so close they were almost touching she could hear the sound of her heartbeat pounding in her ears.

She had to break the tense, pregnant silence. "Alain," she breathed nervously, "you've come home."

"Hello, Fleur." He spoke as if at a first meeting, his glance exploratory, his manner eager, slightly impatient of preliminaries. His mother was right, he had changed. Despite a slight paleness, which was understandable considering his stay in Paris, he exuded a raw vitality, an aura of curbed excitement that was so marked she backed away from him in confusion.

"Are you pleased to see me?" There was devilment in the question; he was playing with her like a cat with a mouse and she resented the cruel torment he so enjoyed inflicting. He was vibrantly happy, of that there was no doubt, but did he have to flaunt his happiness in her face?

Célèstine was probably downstairs waiting for him, ready to discuss ways and means of getting rid of an unwanted wife—a wife both unknown and undesired. The thought, bitter though it was, caused her to tilt her chin with newly aroused pride. He was confident, unaware of the fact that she knew where he had spent the last few weeks, and it was time to enlighten him.

Cool as an April shower, she asked him, "How was Paris?"

She expected him to look shocked, but puzzlement was the overriding expression on his face.

One inquiring black eyebrow tilted questioningly when he repeated: "Paris?"

Nerves in her throat fluttered like a captive bird, and she caught her breath when she charged him, "I know you've spent these past few weeks in Paris with Célèstine! Please don't try to deny it, Alain. You once said—" she bit her lip to steady a quiver "—that you always expect the truth from me. Haven't I the right to expect the same from you?"

She could have sworn his astonishment was genuine. She felt pinned down by the intentness of his look as he stood silently digesting the shock of her words. She backed away from eyes which, though sightless, seemed to bore into the depths of her soul, and was astonished when his hand reached out to snap around her wrist.

"You are adept at jumping to conclusions, are you not, Fleur?" he charged with dangerous softness. "I have not been to Paris. Nor have I had any contact with Célèstine since the day she left the château!"

Her heart threatened to somersault straight out of her body.

"I'm sorry," she gasped. "Perhaps I did jump to a hasty conclusion, but it hardly matters, does it? I know you are in love with Célèstine—I saw her in your room, heard what you said to her. . . ."

When the quiver in her voice turned into a sob, she faltered into silence and turned her head away.

"And the next morning you ran away from me," he challenged with such gentle concern her tear-wet eyes flew immediately to his face. His hand dropped from her wrist. He walked toward the windowseat and sat down. "Come, sit here beside me," he commanded.

She fought to withstand the softly given order, but when she hesitated he demanded forcefully, "Come, Fleur, I want you here!"

She obeyed, but reluctantly. The window-seat was wide and she made toward the opposite end from where he sat, but again he disconcerted her with his uncanny perception by catching hold of her arm and pulling her down beside him. She trembled at his touch, but when he kept her hand a prisoner and began to speak, her trepidation died as she began to listen intently.

"As you are so convinced of my love for Célèstine, it seems I must share with you a secret known only to her and to me." His voice was so devoid of feeling it gave no inkling of what was to come, but she knew by the gravity of his expression that the words came painfully to him.

"It was Célèstine who caused my blindness," he stated simply.

A start of sheer horror jerked through Fleur's body, but she held back the cry that sprang to her lips and waited, wide-eyed with distress, for him to continue. "We were

engaged to be married at the time; an engagement that crept upon us both as it does sometimes with two people who have been thrown
together since childhood and whose family and
friends have come to expect it. In the beginning I did not mind her fits of caprice, her
childish demands for my complete attention;
she was a spoiled child whose word was law to
an indulgent father. But as my interest in the
business grew I found it less and less
convenient to dance attendance upon her, and
the consequent scenes that followed because of
my neglect finally decided me that the engagement should be terminated." He stirred restlessly, reliving the pain of resurrected
memories, and his grip tightened around her
hand, but she was too intent upon his story to
notice pain.

"It happened—" his mouth grew grim
"—on the day I told her of my decision. We
were together in the laboratory. I had finished
my work for the day and had just begun to
clean out the utensils I had been using. Perhaps
I was partly to blame. My mind was occupied
choosing the words I would use to tell her of
my decision and I must have absentmindedly
poured more spirits than I ought into the
cleansing compound. But that is beside the
point," he said with a shrug. "Célèstine lost her

temper. She threw some object toward me and
it dropped into the dish of spirits I was holding,
splashing the contents straight into my eyes."

For long minutes there was silence as he
relived the horror of that moment, and when
she felt the shudder that ran through his body
she knew that never again would she suspect
him of loving Célèstine. Her throat was so
tight with the pain of shame and compassion
that she could barely force out the words.

"Oh, how could she, Alain! How could
anyone . . . ."

When her choked exclamation reached him,
he shook himself free of retrospective thoughts
and brought them both determinedly back to
the present by sliding his arm around her slim
waist and drawing her close against his heart.
"Don't condemn her too much, Fleur," he
whispered against her suddenly fiery cheek. "I
owe her a debt of gratitude I will never be able
to repay."

"Gratitude? How can you speak of gratitude
in connection with Célèstine?"

She was very still within the circle of his
arms, her face hidden against the breadth of
his chest, which was rising and falling with
increased rapidity. A paralyzing shyness held
her. She was afraid to lift her eyes, afraid the

message she might see would not be the one for
which her bewildered heart was searching. His
hand searched for her chin and forced her face
into the open, then he told her, "The night of
the dinner party—the night you saw Célèstine
in my room—I had mistaken her for you,
Fleur." Her reaction to this admission seemed
to be of great importance to him; she felt his
arms tense around her as he waited for her
reply.

"Me? But how . . . ?" she stammered, her
heart racing at the implication behind his
words.

"When I entered my room I heard a rustling noise—the noise I always associate with
the clothes you wear. Also, the perfume I had
devised especially for you, to which, so far as I
was aware, no one else had access, was heavy
in the air. So naturally—"

"You thought they were my arms that
closed around your neck," Fleur added
incredulously.

She was allowed only fleeting seconds to
ponder on the scene, to remember the light tap
of her bedroom door, the stream of light that
had been left as a guide by Célèstine who must
have been waiting in the bathroom for the
sound of Alain's footsteps as he passed on his

way to his room. How cleverly she had fooled them both!

"Fleur!" Alain's urgency was not lost upon her; he was becoming dissatisfied with talk! A thrilling wave of feeling turned her bones to water when she met his glance and remembered the words he had spoken to Célèstine: "My heart's darling! How I have longed to have you back in my arms!"

His eyes glittering down at her sent shivers of delight up and down her spine. He was holding onto his control, waiting until he was sure she understood before attempting to encroach further. "Are there any other of my actions I need to explain?" he jerked out thickly. "Other than those caused by my diabolical moods and my frustrated longing to see the wife whose sweetness had led me once to the very gates of heaven? *Mon Dieu!*" he whispered passionately as his lips hovered fractionally above hers. "If there are they will have to wait. I refuse to be put off a moment longer!"

He kissed her, and her whole body was consumed by a heady, intoxicating wave of desire that rose to meet the passion in his hard, demanding caresses. When their lips met restraint fled, and the hunger in him was gratified by the sweet and utter generosity of her responses.

It was a very long time before he was ready to release her and when he did so it was only to hold her a mere fraction away from him. He looked down at her bemused, rapturous face and whispered, "Fleur, *mon ange, je t'adore!*" Then, he said slowly, "I thought Louis exaggerated when he described your beauty, but he understated, *mon amour.* You are truly the loveliest sight I have ever seen!"

She became very still, registering the implication; then her eyes, startled and pleading, fastened upon the dark glasses that were protecting his eyes.

He removed them, and she was dazzled by the eager, sparkling aliveness that twinkled down at her. She felt the beginnings of an incredulous joy and could not even attempt to force out the question that was clamoring to be asked.

Completely understanding, he smiled and nodded his head as proof he could read the question mirrored in her eyes.

"Yes, Fleur, I can see you! This is the reason I owe a debt of gratitude to Célèstine. When she came to my room that night she stayed only long enough to be told the truth about herself, but in that time I determined that no other arms but yours would ever tempt me; no other lips but yours would ever rest under mine. That was why, as soon as I was sure Maman was out of danger, I went back to the hospital. So you see, my darling, if you want it, I can furnish proof that I was not in Paris!" he teasingly charged her.

She was unable to respond to his quip. The shock he had given her was so intense that she could only grapple with the many emotions that overwhelmed her in swift succession. But he did not intend to wait longer than a minute for her reaction. She just had time to whisper, "Alain, is it really true?" before he swept her up against his heart to kiss her again, long and dynamically, proving once and for all that dreams are mere figments of the imagination and no substitute at all for glorious turbulent reality!

His lovemaking demonstrated the depths of his adoration, and helped to heal the scars upon her heart. But one small part of her still quivered with hurt, one hint of reserve still lingered in the deep recesses of her mind. She knew he was aware of it when he pressed his lips against a pulse that was fluttering in her throat and murmured, "Tell me you love me, Fleur. Let me hear you say it."

"I've always loved you, Alain," she admitted gravely.

"Always?" He held her away and searched for the truth in her steady eyes. She was wildly happy that he had regained his sight, but his added perception made it doubly hard to hide any secret doubts. So she did not try.

Swallowing the fear that his answer might prove more hurtful than her burden of doubt she asked him, "Did you really believe—in the beginning—that my motives for marrying you were mercenary?"

She closed her eyes as she waited for his answer, which was given solemnly and without reservation.

"Never, *ma petite,* I swear it! I pretended to myself that I believed, but only because I was searching for an excuse to take out my own humiliation on you. I had treated you so badly, but much as I regretted having hurt you I cannot be sorry for my actions that night. I came to you full of rage and bitterness and left you with peace and love in my heart."

"You loved me then?" It was a cry from the heart, an echo of a hurt so appalling that he flinched from the realization of the agony he had forced her to endure. Her lashes swept up just in time to meet the torment of remorse in his passion-dark eyes before she was gathered

249

quickly back against his heart. "Yes," he stressed thickly, "I loved you then as I'll love you always, *mon coeur*. I was jealous of Louis, in despair of ever regaining my sight, but nothing could equal the madness I felt at the thought of losing you!"

His mouth closed over hers in a fervor of passion, and within his vital embrace the slender chain that held the blue charm snapped and fell from around her neck. It lay discarded and unnoticed on the floor, only two of the words it contained now relevant: *Unis, toujours!* Together always!

SOUNDINGS

A Thematic Guide
for Daily Scripture Prayer

Rev. Chris Aridas

IMAGE BOOKS
A Division of
Doubleday & Company, Inc.
GARDEN CITY, NEW YORK
1984

Library of Congress Cataloging in Publication Data
Aridas, Chris, 1947–
    Food for the journey.
    1. Meditations.   2. Devotional calendars—Catholic
Church.   3. Catholic Church—Prayer-books and devotions—
English.   I. Title.
BX2182.2.A74   1984   242'.2   83–16509

ISBN: 0-385-19157-X